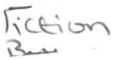

Fun, Frolics and Fandangos with Satire

About the Author

Anna Nolan is a humourist with a penchant for irreverent satire and parody. Besotted with the English language, she is also a linguist specialising in English grammar and the author of several books. Anna worked as a teacher of English, broadcaster at the BBC, manager of public examinations and developer of national qualifications in both England and Scotland. Now retired, she writes, climbs Lakeland mountains and leads a walking group.

Fun, Frolics and Fandangos with Satire

ANNA NOLAN

First published in Great Britain in 2025 by
The Book Guild Ltd
Unit E2 Airfield Business Park,
Harrison Road, Market Harborough,
Leicestershire. LE16 7UL
Tel: 0116 2792299
www.bookguild.co.uk
Email: info@bookguild.co.uk

Copyright © 2025 Anna Nolan

The right of Anna Nolan to be identified as the author of this
work has been asserted by them in accordance with the
Copyright, Design and Patents Act 1988.

All rights reserved. No part of this publication may be
reproduced, transmitted, or stored in a retrieval system, in any form or by any means,
without permission in writing from the publisher, nor be otherwise circulated in
any form of binding or cover other than that in which it is published and without
a similar condition being imposed on the subsequent purchaser.

The manufacturer's authorised representative in the
EU for product safety is Authorised Rep Compliance Ltd,
71 Lower Baggot Street, Dublin D02 P593 Ireland (www.arccompliance.com)

Typeset in 11pt Minion Pro

Printed and bound in Great Britain by 4edge Limited

ISBN 978 1835743 461

British Library Cataloguing in Publication Data.
A catalogue record for this book is available from the British Library.

To Vinnie,

With gratitude for his love, support and encouragement

Two other humorous books by Anna Nolan:

Lakeland Larks, Laughter and Lunacies of an Unmotorised Lake District Walker

and its sequel

More Lakeland Larks, Laughter and Lunacies of a Still Unmotorised Lake District Walker

Contents

1.	High Jinks and Absurdities	1
2.	The Bewildered Meets the Improbable	18
3.	From the Frying Pan Into the Fire	38
4.	Bombshells and Revelations	57
5.	Ploys, Schemes and Strategies	79
6.	Huddles, Aliens and Bombs	99
7.	Moles, Accents, Unconscious Biases and Predictors of Beaconicity	118
8.	Multiple Visions, Solutions-Driven Agendas and the Singapore Takeaway	134
9.	Demigods, Hallucinations and Work-Life Balance of Refuse Collectors	158
10.	The Secret of Waterstones, Uncovering Dalliances and Undressing to Mate	171
11.	Homophones, Flippers, Fishmongers and Casualties	186
12.	Ferrets, Apes and Mongooses	205
13.	Corporate Mayhem, Bombshells, Banquets and Jubilations	221

1

High Jinks and Absurdities

"Fart."

"I beg your pardon?"

"Fart here."

"Just like that?"

"Just like *what?*"

"Well, I am not sure I can manage to... manage it just like that."

"Manage *what?*"

"What you've just told me to do..."

"*You what?*"

"Well, you've just told me to... to... you know."

"I haven't told you to do nothing."

"Well, you did say to... to... to break wind."

"No, no – *fart*; it's, like, what we *are*."

"That's what you *are?*"

"It is."

"Terribly sorry, but I'm not with you."

"That's what we are, like: the Foremost Authority for the Radicalisation of Transformation."

"O-o-o-o, I see: *FART*."

"That's what I've been saying, like."

"Yes, no… I mean it's obviously an acronym."

"No, no, it's an authority, like."

"Yes, no, I meant… oh, never mind. And what do you do exactly?"

"We, like, deliver and stuff."

"You *deliver*? Like in a maternity ward?"

"How do you mean *a maternity ward?*"

"Well, that's what a maternity ward does: delivers babies."

"We don't have no babies here."

"So what do you deliver?"

"Oodles and oodles, like."

"Oodles of *what?*"

After what sounded like a deep sigh at the end of the telephone line, there followed a slight pause, itself followed by some rustling accompanied by several more sighs.

"Just a sec; where's the blinking list? That's it: we deliver revolutionary digital transformation; AI augmented reality paradigms; personalised adaptive digital systems; actionable and practical takeaways for innovative AI solutions; precepts of avoiding inherent algorithmic biases in AI; blueprints for backward propagation in machine learning; transcendental—"

"Good grief, you deliver *all that?*"

"That's what all them people say and stuff. And, like, customer focus."

"And *customer focus?* But what's that about radicalisation? In your name?"

"'Cos we also radicalise and stuff."

"Gosh, you must be busy. You deliver *and* radicalise."

"All the time. And on overtime."

"*And on overtime?* Wow. So you radicalise transformation?"

"That's what all them people say and stuff."

"What sort of transformation exactly?"

"I don't know, do I? They didn't tell me nothing. I'm on work experience here. I'm doing the Comprehensive Certificate in Handling the General Public, like. Stage Two."

"Stage Two?"

"Yaas. Stage Two comes after Stage One, like."

"Does it really?"

"It does, it does! I've, like, got Stage One already."

"Well done. You handle the general public very well."

"That's what all them people say and stuff."

"I'm sure you'll sail through your Stage Two. You've certainly made FA... your organisation sound very intriguing: I'd love to find out more about it. Do you think I could speak to your manager?"

"You could – if he wasn't in a meeting."

"Is he in a meeting?"

"Inco is always in a meeting, like."

"Inco?"

"I mean Mr Inco Herent."

"I see. Maybe I could phone him when he's finished?"

"When he's finished, like, he'll go to another meeting."

"He must be terribly busy."

"That's what all them people say and stuff."

"What about *his* manager? Is he available?"

"She. Nota."

"Nota?"

"Yes, Mrs Nota Clue."

"I see. Is she available?"

"That would be a first, like."

"Would it? Why?"

"Every time Inco is in a meeting, Nota is in the same meeting, like. But she also does extra ones and stuff."

"Dearie me, poor people. Are they foreign, by any chance? They have rather unusual names."

"No, no, they speak English, like."

"Well, I also speak English, but I am foreign."

"But you speak funny, like. But I didn't like to say."

"I'm from Poland."

"Did you come here on a small boat?"

"Good Lord, no! I came here before the Berlin Wall came down."

"It sucks, like."

"*What* sucks?"

"That they had only one wall, like. In Berlin."

"No, no, no, I mean *the* Berlin Wall. It had separated… oh, never mind. Anyway, how could I find out more about FA… about your organisation?"

"Go to our website, like."

"Yes, of course; good idea. The address is…?"

"Www.fart.com."

"Of course, of course, I could have guessed. You've been very helpful."

"No worries. We pride us… ourself on delivering customer focus and stuff."

"Evidently, evidently. Thank you."

"Wait, wait, there is a survey."

"A survey?"

"There's customer satisfaction surveys on our website, like – will you do one about this call and stuff?"

"With pleasure, with pleasure. Good luck with your Stage Two."

***

Actually, I had no intention of approaching the Foremost Authority at all. For a start, I had no idea of its existence. I was merely trying to register for self-employment with our marvellous HMRC. You know how it is: like many other hard-working people our esteemed politicians are so fond of invoking, I had been finding it harder and harder to make my money go as far as it needed to. I mean, keeping myself in all the clobber I have a weakness for doesn't come cheap, does it? What, you thought I had no weaknesses? Even *I* am allowed the odd one. Disappointingly – and, frankly, quite incredibly – the spectacular benefits of Brexit were yet to materialise: Sir Jacob Rees-Mogg said that, for ordinary folk, it would take fifty years. So I decided that I couldn't wait that long. Now, what do you do in similar circumstances? You start a side hustle. Mine was writing books. Not that writing books pays, you know. Not those penned by me anyway. But, being an upstanding citizen, I wouldn't have dreamt of concealing from our tax authorities those few pennies I had earned on the side. I mean, I may be a Slav, but I'm not like Roman Abramovich.

So I tried to log onto the HMRC website. Unfortunately, it was down: apparently, they were in the throes of improving their customer-facing digital connectivity. I then had to resort to an old-fashioned method, using a contraption called a phone. I was greeted by a lengthy recorded message listing a mind-boggling range of things you could do on their website. Given, however, that their website was down, I had no choice but to wait, this being the very last option offered by the disembowelled voice. The way this works is that, rather than pressing any of the buttons enumerated by the voice, you just wait until someone at the other end picks up the phone. That is, assuming it's a human, which you cannot guarantee these days. You then hear the message saying that they are experiencing a large volume of calls and that the wait could be as long as 120 minutes. This makes you hesitate: after all, it's a 0300 number, so, the longer you wait, the more it will cost you. And your books have hardly made you any dough. You then wonder if it's actually a revenue-generating ploy; if the government was prepared to rob pensioners, you couldn't put anything past it, surely.

After two and a half hours of being exposed to soporific music, which, regrettably, isn't to your taste, you are aroused from your torpor by a male voice, which asks how it can help you. Scarcely believing your luck, you explain the purpose of your call. There then follows a comprehensive enquiry whose aim is to establish your identity. Alas, as you are answering the fifteenth security question, the phone goes dead, and no amount of shouting (no swearing, though) seems able to bring it back to life.

Having, however, been taught that perseverance is the key to success – nearly as pivotal as the right connections, that is – you try again, and the previous process is repeated, although, on this occasion, they promise you a wait of 130 minutes. As you finally hear the male voice, you start by pleading not to be disconnected again. The voice, however, isn't promising anything. In any case, you have to go through the security questions first. Full of trepidation, you answer them to the best of your ability. In the end, which you, happily, manage to reach on this occasion, you seem to have convinced the voice that you are you. Elated, you repeat the purpose of your call, whereupon the voice says that you first have to obtain the so-called Gateway User ID. Hopefully, you make a humble supplication to be provided with one, to which the voice replies that this is not how it works.

"How does it work?" you then enquire, your spirits sinking.

The voice says that the only way in which you can achieve your objective is by going online and requesting your Gateway User ID there. Before, however, you have the chance to point out the sheer impossibility of carrying out this injunction, the phone goes dead.

Given that you have already wasted five hours, you are not going to waste any more and decide to give them some time to sort themselves out. Three days later, you visit their website again – only to find that they are continuing to improve their customer-facing digital connectivity. Maybe it's a really big job, you try to reassure yourself as you resolve to give them another week. Needless to say, you are delighted that, on this occasion, the website is up and running – yippee! You then commence the process of registering your request. After successfully performing the required manoeuvres, you are advised that you will receive your government login details through the post within the next ten days. When they do indeed arrive, you can hardly contain your ecstasy: you will now be able to register for self-employment and, in due course, pay the additional tax, although, in your particular case, it is unlikely to be more than £13.50.

It is thus with a certain amount of smugness that you again visit their website and create your password. This, in turn, allows you to enter the personal details required by the government. The next step is to get your access code, and, within a mere few seconds, you do indeed receive an automated call with the code. The lady's voice warns you that the code will expire within the next five minutes, so, when you enter it onto the electronic form, you make sure that you tick the box asking if you want the website to remember this code for the next seven days – you doubt if you will ever need it again, but you never know.

You are then ready to complete your login, but, suddenly, you get an error message saying *You can't view this page*, and you get chucked back to the login section. With a deep sigh, you restart your login, glad that you have asked the website to remember your access code for the next seven days. When the website instructs you to request another access code, you know that it has already forgotten the old one. So you are not entirely clear why you *again* ask the website to remember you access code for the next seven days, but human beings are not always rational. Another access code arrives by phone, you enter it and… the screen displays the unnerving message saying *Oops, something went wrong.* Having again been chucked back to the login section, you feel like screaming (and perhaps even swearing), but what choice have you got?

You thus repeat the entire manoeuvre, including requesting yet another access code from the forgetful website, and... you are in! Scarcely believing your luck, you enter all the personal details relevant to your application, including your home address, but the website isn't buying it: you are duly informed that the address you have entered 'doesn't match our records'. But you have lived at this very address for over twenty-five years and know it off by heart. Nothing doing, however.

Desperate by this point, you feel that you have no option but to call the HRMC again. I will, of course, spare you the details of how this goes initially, but, when you finally hear a female voice – after a mere ninety minutes this time – you are informed that you have called the wrong department: they are all tax experts there (hmmm, with £5 billion in uncollected tax being written off in 2023/2024?). According to the voice, the people you want are the technical department. Hoping that your tone doesn't betray your feelings, you ask how to get hold of the people from the technical department, and the voice helpfully says that it will put you through. You wonder how long you will have to endure the soporific tunes, but it's only half an hour. You then explain your predicament, whereupon the new voice enquires if you are absolutely sure that you have entered the right address. You swear on your life that you are and that you have, to which the new voice retorts that it finds it very strange and that it will have to speak to its supervisor. You then enquire, albeit weakly, if you could have the supervisor's phone number so that you might be able to speak to this person yourself, to which the answer is a firm negative. But the voice reassures you that it will call you back within the next hour – unless said supervisor is working from home, of course – and then promptly cuts you off.

After four hours have elapsed and you still haven't been called back, you make your final, desperate, bid and phone the tax people again on the number you do have. And it is then that you misdial the number – easily done, particularly if you are in the state you are in. This is exactly what happened to me on that fateful day when I inadvertently got through to FART.

***

FART's website revealed a wealth of riveting information, confirming that the helpful work-experience girl was spot on about delivery. Among many other eye-catching things which FART seemed to be delivering were:

- *Transcendental Possibilities in the Digital Transformation of Key Education and Training Missions, Visions, Principals, Policies, Pledges, Priorities, Initiatives and Strategies* (I suspected they meant *principles*, although I couldn't be entirely sure, of course);
- *The AI Radicalisation of the New Employer Focused Skills Revolution to Penetrate the Governmental Growth and Productivity Agenda* (I wondered if you could penetrate an agenda. And also why nobody at FART spotted that the necessary hyphen with the compound *employer-focused* had done a runner);
- *Relentless Focus on Revolutionising the Civil Societys Covenant Framework for the Nations Renewal and*

Greatness (this sounded a bit Trumpian to me. And, since both apostrophes had gone AWOL, I was unable to establish whether FART was concerned with only one society and nation or, perhaps, several of them).

The aforementioned misgivings on my part notwithstanding, I was transfixed. And the more I read, the harder it became to picture FART as anything other than a huge delivery room. But there appeared to be more to the Foremost Authority than delivering, for, among its other riveting activities, the website listed:

- *Championing the Embedding and Enhancing of Transformational Synergies and Blueprints and Inherent Innovative Capacities of AI;*
- *Unleashing Revolutionary Digital Radicalisation of a 'Second Horizon' Transition Strategy in Education and Training to deliver the Economic Miracle* (how many horizons were there in education, I wondered. And could you actually radicalise one?);
- *Persuing Digital Training Blueprints, Paradigms, Schemes and Strategies for Unassailable Dominance on the World Stage* (the more I read, the more I wondered whether the Authority was in-between proofreaders. Or perhaps its spellchecker had packed up. You can't always trust modern technology. But the Trumpian influences were definitely there).

While my scrutiny of the website failed to establish with any degree of certainty what it was *exactly* that FART did, it was nevertheless obvious that the radicalisation and transformation in its title had something to do with both education and AI. And perhaps an economic miracle. Now, that was a line of enquiry worth pursuing further. In these straitened times, we could do with an economic miracle, no question about it. So, if FART could help us out there, it was certainly worth finding out about. Besides, I've been told that AI is the only game in town. Obviously, I myself wouldn't know, but, unlike a segment of the population, I do believe in experts. Not the self-proclaimed ones off TikTok: the real ones – I do listen to Radio 4 and read *The Economist*. As a person with congenital investigative leanings, I thus decided there and then to plunge headlong into the somewhat baffling, yet tantalising, world of the Foremost Authority. I guessed that a section called Foremost Opportunities contained information on FART's vacancies.

I was correct: when I clicked on Foremost Opportunities, I could see that they had a few vacancies going. At this juncture, I must confess to a certain – OK, OK, a substantial – amount of vanity: I had always wanted to have a grand-sounding job title. Disappointingly, it had, thus far, eluded me, all my previous titles being decidedly pedestrian. I mean what's special about being called a teacher? Or a copy editor? Or a manager of exams? Or, for that matter, a developer of qualifications? Or even a broadcaster at the Polish Section of the BBC? They are all ten a penny. Well, maybe not the last one: when I worked in London for the Polish Section of the BBC way back when, there weren't all that many of us, but the world is practically littered with the others. So this was my opportunity to end my professional career with a bang. Besides, one must seize every opportunity life throws one's way – particularly if one comes from Poland. But even though you have been blessed with the good fortune of being born in Britain, would you *yourself* be able to resist the allure of the title which caught my eye? It went like this:

> Premier Adviser on the Inherent Innovative
> Capacities of AI in the Radicalisation of
> Transformation in Education

Come on, admit it: you'd love to be called Premier Adviser on all these things, wouldn't you? Be truthful.

But when I looked at the person specification for the job, my heart sank. The person they wanted would have to be a highly motivated and self-aware self-starter, a hard-hitting communicator and a sharp-witted decision-maker with a growth mindset and insatiable curiosity who is able to spin multiple plates, reach even the highest-hanging fruit and set a visionary road map for the radicalisation of transformation in education to deliver unstoppable economic growth. Moreover, they would need to be a strong and inspirational leader with an unwavering dedication to life-long learning who is able to keep abreast of, and even anticipate, trends and advances in both education and digital technology and who exhibits an unbridled passion for AI and a demonstrable ability to drive through governmental policies, pledges, priorities, missions, visions, initiatives and strategies in the relentless pursuit of the economic miracle and the promised post-Brexit sunlit uplands.

Bummer: I could just see this unique opportunity slipping right through my fingers. But when I shared my disappointment with a savvy friend, she started laughing uncontrollably. My pride having been somewhat hurt, I cooly enquired as to what exactly was so funny about my – entirely justifiable – misgivings: I knew next to nothing about AI, wasn't good at spinning, had no head for heights so couldn't pick anything hanging high, don't like hitting people – even lightly – and am rather adept at procrastination. Then again, my Polish passions could, indeed, be unbridled, and I am always very curious about what other folk are up to, so maybe I did stand a chance, after all. Anyway, when she finally stopped laughing and regained her composure, she said to go for it, assuring me that I would be absolutely fine before erupting into another fit of giggles. I had to wait a bit until normal proceedings could be resumed, whereupon she instructed me to paraphrase every single bit mentioned in the person specification while stressing that I was fully aware that AI was the only game in town. Well, at least I had heard this stuff from others, so it must be true. Not that the objective truth exists anyway: ask Donald Trump.

She then said that I would have to enlarge on all the profound and lasting impacts I had made in my previous role. In my previous role, however, I was one of the developers of the Scottish Curriculum for Excellence, but the initiative ended in disaster, educational attainment in Scotland having plummeted as a result of the Scottish government's reckless experiment with sacrificing knowledge at the altar of ill-defined skills. So, again, I could see the opportunity of acquiring a fancy job title slipping away. My friend, however, remained upbeat, being familiar with my employment history.

"Look, you could see the folly of the whole Scottish thing."

"I could indeed."

"So you resigned in disgust before the end of your contract."

"I did indeed. And, in my exit questionnaire, I told them exactly what I thought about the whole shebang."

"There you go. So just gloss over your Scottish experience and highlight your other impacts."

"Such as editing all these books and articles, which were riddled with grammatical, punctuation and spelling errors, and making them clear and readable?"

"That's it, that's it!"

She then told me that, on the application form, I also had to say that I am a cultivated and passionate professional whose natural intellectual curiosity and growth mindset have fuelled my stratospheric employment progress, that one of my key qualities was penetrating self-awareness, which made me uniquely suitable for the position being advertised, and that I profoundly identified with FART's corporate culture and all its values, principles, missions, visions, blueprints, policies, priorities, objectives, pledges, initiatives and strategies, about which I simply couldn't wait to learn even more and the implementation of which would constitute the absolute pinnacle in my professional career. Oh, and targets. And to say that my one and only weakness was perfectionism.

Despite my misgivings, which my friend hadn't quite managed to dispel, I did decide to give it a go. After all, who could resist the appeal of working in an extremely fast-paced, forward-looking and innovative organisation dedicatedly investing in all its employees, relentlessly pushing the boundaries of innovation and expanding the frontiers thereof as well as determinately driving through transformative change? At least that was what their website said they were. Similarly irresistible looked the manifold benefits of the role: an extremely rewarding, challenging and motivating experience; an invaluable learning curve and a unique development opportunity; a remarkably personally fulfilling and professionally valuable role utilising and enhancing many transferable skills; an unparalleled scope for harnessing your talents, expertise and energy to create high-performing and dynamic teams; an unsurpassed chance to make a genuine difference and to engineer an economic miracle. Stuff like this.

And don't even get me started on the perks! Apparently, FART offered an unrivalled range of employee benefits, including a wide assortment of wellness programmes and well-being tools and strategies; frequent motivational activities; corporate bonding awaydays; flexible working; significant work/life balance; the subsidised canteen and free working breakfasts, lunches and dinners – to name only the most alluring ones. Having digested all of this, I simply knew I had to apply.

The application form – a bit on the long side, it has to be said – was accompanied by the Equalities, Opportunities, Diversity and Inclusion Form and ten appendices. Appendix 1 said, 'How to Gather the Evidence for this Application', Appendix 2 said, 'How to Read this Application Form', Appendix 3 said, 'How to Interpret this Application Form', Appendix 4 said, 'How to Complete this Application Form', Appendix 5 said, 'How to Read the Equalities, Opportunities, Diversity and Inclusion Form', Appendix 6 said, 'How to Interpret the Equalities, Opportunities, Diversity and Inclusion Form', Appendix 7 said, 'How to Complete the Equalities, Opportunities, Diversity and Inclusion Form', Appendix 8 said, 'The Application Form Checklist', Appendix 9 said, 'The Equalities, Opportunities, Diversity and Inclusion Form Checklist' and Appendix 10 said, 'What Happens Next'.

While the volume of the whole shebang was substantial, we Poles are not easily daunted. After all, we vanquished the Turks, repelled the Swedes, stood up to the Germans and outmanoeuvred the Russians, so what's one British application pack to an indomitable Pole – even if it does run to eighty-seven pages? And, anyway, both the form itself and the appendices were most illuminating, confirming that the authority was in dire need of a professional copy editor and proofreader, and I was sure that I could help them out there.

2

The Bewildered Meets the Improbable

"Hello and welcome to our organisation," said the lady from the UHP. When I received the letter offering me the job, I was somewhat mystified by this acronym. Could it have meant *Ultra High Power*? After all, everything about FART seemed to project an image of a very powerful organisation. But it could also have meant *Ultra High Performance*, what with all this radicalising, unleashing, harnessing and championing. And delivery, of course. After a while, however, I decided that it was more likely to refer to *Universal Hiring Programme*. In a way, I was glad that they hadn't spelt the entire title out: I bet they would have written *Program*. Doesn't it just drive you mad to see American spellings everywhere? I mean, I love America and everything, don't get me wrong. Our dearest friend, Bob, is American, after all, and he epitomises all that is great about that country. No, I don't mean great as in Trump & Co – I mean great as in principled, ethical, honest, respectful, things like that. It subsequently transpired, however, that, at FART, UHP stood for *Unleashing Human Potential.*

I bet you are wondering how I got the job in the first place. If truth be told, so am I. But I had followed my friend's advice to the letter, and, after I sent off my application, I spent many days memorising its contents until I was practically word perfect. I also practised radiating passion, enthusiasm, dynamism, strength, drive, vision, vibrancy and energy as well as an unshakeable commitment to the transformational powers of AI. Actually, passion and enthusiasm are inherent Polish traits, so I didn't have to rehearse too hard, but the other stuff I had to work at. In the end, I was able to project all this with such conviction that it must have overridden their natural doubts. I mean, you recruit in your own image, don't you? No, you don't necessarily do this consciously, but that's how it is. They call it an unconscious bias. Actually, my savvy friend said that this is exactly why organisations – particularly those in the public sector – must have comprehensive diversity, inclusion and equal opportunities policies. At least 305 pages long. Of course, nobody reads the bumf, and senior staff keep happily recruiting in their own image. But the point is that, if they should ever be challenged, they would be able to hide behind those policies. Who can argue with 305 pages? In small print.

So here I was – right on the threshold of a brand-new frontier, poised to penetrate transformational innovation and to nail AI right into the veins of the nation. Actually, I doubt if frontiers have thresholds or if you can penetrate innovation. Or, for that matter, if AI is nailable, so I had better take all of this stuff back. But, you see, I am writing this after I have been employed by FART for what seemed like an eternity, so it's inevitable that at least some of its idiosyncrasies, proclivities, singularities, penchants and mannerisms – including their proclivity for tautology – should have left their mark on me. But it took a while, so, as I am recounting the events here, I am sure you will be able to catch a few glimpses of the old me – not that the picture is necessarily that much more flattering.

I had spent the short wait for the UHP lady in the plush reception area chatting amiably with Chardonnay, the helpful work-experience girl who prided herself on delivering customer focus and stuff. It turned out that she remembered our telephone conversation quite vividly.

"Funny accent. I could tell you was not like them other people who call and stuff. Even before you told me you was from Poland, like."

Well, the remedial-grammar people will certainly have their work cut out, I reflected. Actually, do they do remedial grammar in British colleges? Much as I would have liked to ponder this question for a little while, good manners required that I give my interlocutor my undivided attention: our causerie was flowing like a cascading Lakeland stream.

"There's many Poles where I live, like."

"Yes, there are many of us here. It's a very welcoming country, Britain."

"There's lots of Polish shops as well. Dank."

"Oh dear, how unpleasant."

"*You what?*"

"Well, you've just said that the Polish shops are damp and cold."

"No, I didn't: I said *dank*, like."

"That's what I mean."

"No, no, *legit*, like."

"I'm sure these Polish shops are legitimate: we are all settled here legally, you know."

"No, *bussin'*, *bangin'*, *crackin'*, like!"

"You mean *good?*"

"Bet. But good is, like, old-fashioned. It's for old people. Like you. But you can say 'hella good.'"

"That's good, I mean hella good, Chardonnay."

"You can call me Chard, if you like."

"Thank you, Chard. So why are these shops good – I mean dank?"

"They do them kabanos sausages and stuff."

"Ummm, it's UPF, though."

"What's UPF?"

"Ultra-Processed Food. Not very good for you."

The girl shot me a highly doubtful look and shook her head vigorously, but, then, rather than pursuing what she clearly thought would be an unavailing line of enquiry, she swerved our conversation – most diplomatically, I thought. Actually, I wouldn't be surprised if she aced her Stage Two – her idiosyncratic grammar notwithstanding.

"Do you like it here?"

"I love it, absolutely love it here, Chard. It's a wonderful country."

"Is it really? It rains buckets, though. How often do you go home, like?"

"Every day."

"Can you, like, commute from Poland?"

"Well, England *is* my home, Chard; I've lived here for many years, you know."

"I, like, meant *Poland*."

"I know, I know; every now and then."

It was at this juncture that I was swiftly intercepted by the UHP lady, who said, "Let me introduce you to the colleagues from your cluster. This way, please." Having navigated several flights of stairs – the lift wasn't working for some reason – we entered a large open-plan office with rows of desks facing each other and a computer on each. The walls were lined with shelves full of hefty folders. My future colleagues stopped in their tracks and looked at me.

"This is... sorry, how do you pronounce your name again?" asked the UHP lady.

"Szczodra," I said with some trepidation, which was, regrettably, always entirely justified. My forename is indeed most unfortunate. It is unusual even by Polish standards, and, of course, it is completely unpronounceable to the natives. My dear parents (may they rest in peace) decided to call me 'generous' – which is the meaning of Szczodra – totally unaware that lady luck would single me out for seriously preferential treatment and would, in due course, pack me off to Britain, modestly hiding its greatness behind the white cliffs of Dover.

"Shodra, this is Aston. Aston Ishing."

"Pleased to meet you, Mr Ishing."

"Aston, Aston, please. You too, Sho... Zho... Zodra."

"Aston is the CH here."

"You mean the Companion of Honour?"

"No, no, I mean the Cluster Head. Of *your* cluster here."

"Yes, of course. It's always best if a cluster has a head."

"It is, it is. Aston will be your mentor during your probationary period."

The looks I continued to direct at him were meant to furnish me with a general idea as to what sort of person he might be: you know that first impressions are formed in the few initial seconds of each encounter, don't you? On the other hand, I didn't want to appear too forthright: you don't want to take any chances with your mentor. So I settled on a series of side-glances, in between which I would modestly lower my eyes in order to look decorous. And deciding on a smile in similar circumstances is also always tricky: it mustn't be wide, but it must be discernible. I thus quickly opted for one along the lines of Mona Lisa's, hoping that it didn't look too insipid.

Aston had an imposing frame and a drooping moustache. The top of his head was bald, but the sides had sprouted clumps of greying hair. His in-tray was overflowing with papers, on top of which, balancing precariously, sat a plate piled high with chocolate digestives.

"Welcome to our League of Nations."

"League of Nations?"

"Basically, we have all sorts of nationalities here; you'll fit in."

"I hope so, Aston; I am a bit apprehensive – I suppose it's only—"

"No need to worry, Zorba; you'll be fine. I'll be your mentor, you know what I'm saying. It's one of my priority deliverables for this quarter."

As if to demonstrate his mentoring prowess, Aston deftly deployed what he undoubtedly thought would be an excellent icebreaker, although, from my perspective, it rather lacked in originality.

"Do you like it here, Shurba?"

"I love it, absolutely love it here, Aston. It's a wonderful country."

"Is it? If you ask me, it's a bit on the draughty side, you know what I'm saying."

"Yes, I've noticed."

"How often do you go home?"

"Every day."

"How do you mean?"

"Sorry, Aston: it's my little joke. I've lived here a long time, so it feels like home."

"I meant Poland."

"I know, I know; every now and then."

"Jolly good. Have a biscuit."

"Thanks, Aston; maybe a bit later."

The UHP lady now turned to a young female with a pleasant round face, whose desk was facing Aston's. She was just finishing a biscuit, which looked like one of his, and was wiping her chocolate-smeared lips with her hand.

"This is Dali-Ance. Dali-Ance supports Aston."

"Pleased to meet you, Dali-Ance. You have a very… very interesting name."

"Bet. Me mum, she deffo fancied it when she 'eard it."

"Where did she hear it?"

"In the 'ospital where I were born."

"Oh, yes?"

"They asked her 'bout me dad, like."

"So what did she say, Dali-Ance?"

"That she didn't 'ave no clue who the dude was, innit?"

"And?"

"They 'elped her with me name."

"How exactly?"

"They said somynk 'bout Dali-Ance, like, and me mum fought it were Gucci."

"You mean nice?"

"Bet."

"Yes, it's a… it's a very… very… evocative name, Dali-Ance."

"But you can call me Dali: they all do, innit?"

"You are packed quite tightly in here, aren't you, Dali? There isn't much room to spread your papers." I looked at Aston's overflowing in-tray.

"No kiddin', like. They don' want us to 'ave no papers – there's no room for nuffink, like. Proper mingin'."

"So you manage to do everything on screen, Dali?"

"You jokin' me!"

At this point, Aston, looking slightly annoyed, decided to intercede. "That's enough, Dali; thank you. I am Shodra's mentor, you know what I'm saying." He then turned to the UHP lady: "Thank you, Fata, I will handle the rest of the introductions myself. Zorda is in very safe hands."

"I'm sure she is, Aston. I will love you and leave you, then."

With this, the UHP lady – her name was Mrs Fata Morgana – made for the door, and Aston took over effortlessly.

"Zorda, we can't do everything on screen: we do lots of meetings, you know what I'm saying."

"Yes, yes, Chardonnay did say. About Nota and Inco."

"Nah, it's not just them: we *all* do lots of meetings.

Basically, that's why we decided to start you today: only half of us are in meetings."

"A very good idea, Aston."

"Anyways, we need lots of bumf for meetings. So we have to print tons of the stuff off, right?"

"But where do you put it when you are finished with it?"

"We shred it. In this day and age, you can't be too careful, right?"

"You can't?"

"Absolutely not – not if you are working in radicalisation and transformation, you know what I am saying. The stuff is highly sensitive."

"And if you ever need to work on it again – what happens then?"

Aston looked at me as if I had just landed from Mars. "We print it off again. Obviously."

"So then you have to shred it *again?*"

"Absolutely."

"You must get through a lot of paper."

"And shredders, you know what I am saying, and shredders. But our procurement department, they are top notch."

"We have a procurement department?"

"Obviously. Stu Peed and Ana Vailing, they know their stuff. You have a lot to learn, Shorda. We might as well start now. What is the most important principle of procurement?"

"To get the best value for money?"

"That too, but I mean the *most* important?"

"To ensure that you allow all relevant suppliers – not

just your chums – to submit their bids? It was awful, what happened during the Covid pandemic: Michael Gove just opened the chequebook, and the likes of Michelle Mone went to town. Sixty million is an awful lot of money."

"But that's also about value for money, Shodra. Nah, I meant equality, diversity and inclusion, you know what I'm saying."

"*Equality, diversity and inclusion?*"

"Absolutely. Your suppliers must have sound equality, diversity and inclusion policies, you know what I am saying. That's the first thing Stu and Ana scrutinise, right? And all the processes these suppliers follow to ensure that their policies are fully implemented."

"I... I... I don't know what to say, Aston."

"You don't need to say anything. Just listen and learn, you know what I'm saying."

Yes, there was no doubt that getting to grips with how things were done at FART would be quite an education. I looked at the shelves lining the walls.

"What's on these shelves, Aston?"

"Statutes, directives, policies, rules, regulations, guidelines, instructions, circulars, handbooks, schedules, specifications, exhortations, stuff like that."

"Gosh, that's rather a lot. But how come you haven't shredded them?"

"Because we have to follow the stuff, right? It's not ours: it comes from our sponsoring government department."

"We have a sponsoring government department?"

There was no disguising the look of exasperation on Aston's face. "*Of course* we have a sponsoring government department, Shodra. How do you think we are funded?"

"I... I... I never thought about funding."

"*You never thought about funding?* Funding is the *first* thing you think about, right? *Always.* Remember this."

"I will, I will, Aston. So how do they fund us?"

"Basically, they give us a grant: we are a quango."

"A quango?"

"Yup, a quasi-autonomous non-governmental organisation, right?"

"So which government department sponsors us?"

"Department for the Digital Revolution."

"*Department for the Digital Revolution?* I've never heard of it."

"You wouldn't: it's fairly new, right?"

"I see."

"But there was a bloodbath before it was created, you know what I am saying."

"Proper mingin'!" exclaimed Dali, who was evidently listening to our conversation, what with her sitting right opposite Aston.

"*A bloodbath*, Aston?"

"Yup, Shorba, right at the heart of the government. We had the Department for Education and the Department for Science, Innovation & Technology squabbling over which one should control us, right? They couldn't agree for ages, so, in the end, it was decided to set up a brand-new one."

"And the new department managed to issue all these statutes, directives, policies, rules, regulations and... and things?"

"Yup, they are very good like that, you know what I'm saying. I've been told that, if you want to get a job in government, they test you on how quickly you can produce stuff like this."

"I... I... I don't know what to say."

"No probs. Just listen and learn, listen and learn, you know what I'm saying. Anyways, we have proper training lined up for you, so let's return to introductions."

Aston turned towards another young girl – maybe even younger than Dali, next to whom she was sitting. This one had a ponytail and cute freckles, the latter concentrating on her cheeks and nose.

"Meet Dew. Dew is Welsh."

"Hello, Shodra – did I get it right?"

"Close enough, Dew; nice to meet you." Touched by the girl's concern not to mispronounce my name, I gave her a warm smile, and she reciprocated, her freckled nose wrinkling as she smiled. I thought it was nice that they... that we had young people working here. After all, they are our future. And you feel younger in their company, don't you? Aston then outstretched his arm towards an older lady with glasses sitting at a nearby desk.

"Meet Crystal; Crystal is from Denmark."

"Welcome, Zhod... sorry, what was it again?"

"Szczodra. I'm glad I don't have to worry about pronouncing *your* name, Crystal: nice and easy."

"It is. We spell it Kristal at home, but when in Rome..."

"That's what I always say myself."

Like me, Crystal spoke with a foreign accent – although definitely less pronounced, my strenuous efforts to make my enunciation resemble that of Jacob Rees-Mogg having failed rather miserably. But when people also speak with a foreign accent – even when theirs is better than yours –

you can't help feeling a certain affinity towards them, can you?

"Crystal is our Chief Adviser on the Inherent Innovative Capacities of AI in the Radicalisation of Transformation in Education, Zhadra," continued Aston.

"Like me?"

"Nah, you are Premier Adviser, you know what I'm saying."

"What's the difference?"

"The Chief Adviser grade is two rungs up from yours. And I'm Supreme Adviser – that's *three* rungs up, right?"

"But they are… they are all synonyms, Aston."

"Nah, we don't believe in synonyms here, Sharda. We also have Principal Advisers and Foremost Advisers, right? The Principal ones are the second up, and the Foremost ones are the highest."

"Are you saying that I'm *the lowest*, Aston?"

"Of course you are the lowest, Zarda; what did you expect? You've only just started."

I was shattered: there I was, thinking that I had finally reached the dizzying pinnacle of corporate success – only to be cruelly disabused of the notion. But I knew I had to conceal my disillusionment lest they thought I had ideas above my station. Which I did.

"Yes, yes, naturally, Aston. Nevertheless, that's a lot… a lot of Adviser grades, don't you think?"

"A lot? Nah – only five. We also have five Enthuser grades, you know what I'm saying."

"*Enthuser?*"

"Yup. Enthusers are above Advisers, right? Nota and Inco – have you heard about them?"

"Yes, yes, Chardonnay did mention them."

"Jolly good; Nota and Inco are Enthusers. In other departments, this grade is called Director – but *not* in ours, right?" The tone of his voice seemed to suggest that he thought we were somehow special, and I decided to sound impressed.

"Wow."

"And we have five administrative and five clerical grades, right? Below us – obviously. They are our life support."

"Do we need life support here, Aston?"

"It often feels like that, ha, ha, ha!" Crystal's chuckle made her face light up.

"But… but I thought organisations were moving towards flatter management structures."

"Not here, they are not. They may be in the *private* sector, but a fat lot of good it did them: British economy is practically stagnant, and we've got a productivity crisis, you know what I'm saying. Besides, if you have a flatter management structure, how are you going to progress?"

"Well, people can progress sideways…"

"Not here, they cannot. Anyways, everybody is happy with how things are here, right? Apart from Millie."

"Who's Millie?"

"Millie Tant. She is in a meeting but should be back soon."

"Her desk is opposite mine, Shubra," said Crystal, who, I thought, was trying to stifle another chuckle. "And you are sitting next to me. That's your desk here."

The empty desk she was pointing at was sitting between hers and Aston's, and I hoped that I would have an ally on one side at least. Obviously, I didn't know Crystal, but there was something about her bespectacled face and mischievous smile that lifted my spirits – if only a little.

"That's great, Crystal. You can show me the ropes."

"If you don't mind, Zorba, *I* will show you the ropes: I'm your mentor here – *not* Crystal, you know what I'm saying." Aston appeared somewhat irked.

"Terribly sorry, Aston; of course, of course: *you* will show me the ropes."

"I will indeed, Sharda, I will indeed." Aston turned to Crystal. "Is that clear?"

"Crystal clear," replied Crystal with a barely perceptible smile.

It was clearly time to terminate my pleasantries with her, and, as I looked at Aston, I ensured that my physiognomy continued to reflect a blend of concentration and deference: you don't want to fall out with your mentor on the very first day in the office, do you?

"Basically, Zubra, there's a few more of us in our cluster; I'll introduce you when they get back to the office. Anyways, I have to look at the latest bumf from our R&D now."

"R&D?"

"Yup, Research and Development Department."

"We have a Research and Development Department? But we are not an industry – not like computing, engineering or pharmaceuticals, for example. It's not as if we are going to patent anything, surely?"

"Nah, but we do churn out bumf on an industrial scale, right?"

"We do?"

"We do indeed, we do indeed. Do you know how much

effort goes into keeping up with all the constant chopping and changing?"

"Of what?"

"Of governmental policies, of course. So we have to do heaps of research into the way the wind blows at any given moment. And political winds change more often than those driven by our Atlantic lows."

"They do?"

"They do indeed, they do indeed. So we have to keep an eye on all the political vagaries. A weather eye – so to speak. And then we have to develop strategies to accommodate those vagaries. That's why we must have an R&D Department, you know what I'm saying."

"We must, we *absolutely* must, Aston!" As you can see, I was now utterly convinced.

He nodded, clearly pleased with his obvious mentoring prowess. "Actually, ours is planning an expansion and has been recruiting recently."

This made me slightly uneasy. "Isn't everybody recruiting, Aston?"

"So?"

"We may not get the best talent."

"We weren't going to get the best talent anyway."

"Oh?"

"Basically, the best talent wants to work in investment banking, data science, engineering, marketing, plastic surgery – particularly private, things like that."

"I s-e-e-e-e."

"And we had to replace Eva; we'd lost her."

"She went to work in investment banking?"

"Nah, she had a nervous breakdown."

"How awful!"

"Yup; Eva Cuation was in charge of all the bumf they had to keep coming up with in our R&D. They made her research, and then produce our response to, all these overarching governmental protocols and forecasts, predictors of beaconicity in public life, stakeholder toolkits for process-driven gateway reviews, horizon—"

"Good grief!"

"Let me finish please: horizon scanning for interdepartmental interface, policy directives and regulatory exhortations for rebaselining, core principles of cross-fertilisation—"

"I didn't know we dealt with agriculture as well, Aston."

"*Agriculture?*"

"Well, this cross-fertilisation—"

"No, no, no, it's about cross-fertilisation of visions, missions, purposes, ideas, designs, recommendations, goals, things like that. So poor Eva, she had a lot on her plate. And they were giving her these tight deadlines: government policy can change more quickly than a cheetah in full flow. So she was getting more and more stressed, right?"

"Is this why she had a nervous breakdown?"

"No, not exactly: she was very resilient. What finished her off were our wellness programmes, you know what I'm saying."

"*Our wellness programmes?*"

"Yup. Basically, FART offers all sorts: mindfulness sessions, meditation courses, serenity counselling, brain massage, laughing therapy. It's all about stress management, right?"

"Well, it… it certainly is… is mind-blowing. But

how could our wellness programmes have *possibly* given anybody a nervous breakdown?"

"After Eva and Penny were discharged from hospital—"

"Who is Penny?"

"Penny Pincher worked in our Finance Department. She also had a nervous breakdown."

"Did they *both* have to be hospitalised?"

"Yup, for months."

"Good grief! So what happened after they were discharged?"

"Basically, they were interviewed. At length, right?"

"So what did they say?"

"Before her breakdown, Eva had apparently complained of feeling stressed, so our R&D Director decided to send her on a stress management course."

"And did it help?"

"Nah, not really. So they sent her on more stress management courses, right?"

"And they didn't help either?"

"Too right, they didn't – they did the opposite, you know what I'm saying."

"In what way?"

"Basically, people running these courses kept telling her that, on completion, she would feel less stressed."

"And did she?"

"Nah: she actually felt *more* stressed because she kept getting further and further behind with her work."

"Really?"

"She did indeed, she did indeed. Think about it, Shorda: all these wellness programmes would take quite a chunk out of her working day, right?"

"I suppose."

"So she ended up having less and less time for her actual work. And all these overarching governmental protocols and forecasts, predictors of beaconicity in public life, stakeholder toolkits for process-driven gateway reviews, horizon scanning for interdepartmental interface, policy directives and regulatory exhortations for rebaselining and core principles of cross-fertilisation she was having to research and formulate a response to – they didn't get any less challenging. Or any less numerous, you know what I'm saying."

"Hmm, I suppose."

"So she ended up feeling even worse than she had done before she started attending all these wellness programmes, right? Besides, she had the *additional* stress of realising that she had failed to solve the problem of being stressed by *the initial* problem."

"Oh, dear, poor Eva. So what did this Penny from Finance have to say?"

"Much the same, although she had been snowed under with all sorts of financial statements and logs, ledgers, balance sheets, record books – things like that. But she said that the worst thing was having to conceal the full scale of our expenditure."

"Did she really have to do this?"

"Think about it: with all the austerity under the Tories, hospitals, prisons and homes weren't being built, public services were being cut to the bone, local authorities were on their knees, people were feeling the pinch and here we were, spending their hard-earned moolah on horizon scanning and the like. So they told her she had to be creative with our financial accounting. And when she buckled, they sent her on a stress management course."

"But it didn't work for her either?"

"Look, Zorda, I've told you that these wellness programmes are a waste of time."

"So why do our managers keep sending people on them?"

"To cover their back."

"Oh?"

"They use these programmes to pretend that they care about their employees, right?"

"But they don't?"

"What do you reckon?"

"My goodness, perhaps I shouldn't have applied for this job, after all…"

"Look, Zadra, it's the same wherever you work. Basically, in this day and age, people are quick to complain or sue, you know what I'm saying. So their employers daren't take any chances. Whether these courses work or not is immaterial, right?"

"Perhaps we need a wellness course designed to reduce the stress caused by wellness courses, ha, ha, ha!" Crystal had obviously been listening to our exchange.

"Perhaps we do… Anyways, I need to look at this R&D stuff now. Go and get some coffee, and you can get me a cup as well: no milk, four sugars. Crystal, would you show Shodra where the kitchenette is, please."

3

From the Frying Pan Into the Fire

The kitchenette – on the spacious side, it has to be said – occupied a corner of our floor. In addition to the usual kitchen stuff, there were several tables there, each with a cluster of chairs, a comfortable-looking, cushion-strewn, sofa accompanied by a coffee table and three brightly coloured space hoppers.

"Wow, this looks more like a lounge than a kitchenette, Crystal."

"It does, it does. We use it for meetings when we have run out of meeting rooms."

"Do we run out of meeting rooms very often?"

"All the time."

"I see. Aston did say that you… that we do lots of meetings. But why do you… we have these space hoppers?"

"For bouncing around."

"Why would you want to bounce around in the office?"

"They say it's to release tension whenever you are stressed. We are very hot on all sorts of well-being strategies. Aston has just told you all about our wellness programmes, hasn't he? Ha, ha, ha!"

"He has, he has, but I can't say I have found the stuff particularly reassuring. I hope they won't send me on one."

"So, whatever you do, don't mention your mental health. As soon as people complain about their mental health, it's all action stations."

"It wouldn't even cross my mind, Crystal. I mean, you just deal with the difficulties and disappointments life throws at you, don't you? Or all the sadnesses. I mean, it's part and parcel of life, isn't it?"

"Of course. But, nowadays, there seems to be this tendency to medicalise everything. So don't give them the chance."

"I won't, I won't, Crystal."

"Anyway, I wasn't talking about wellness *programmes* as such. Millie had been badgering our senior management to introduce all sorts of well-being *strategies* here so that everyone could benefit."

"For example?"

"These space hoppers you've asked me about. She got them for us."

"You mean the Millie who was unhappy about our hierarchical structure? According to Aston?"

"The very same, the very same. She is very active in fighting for our rights. But she can go over the top."

"What do you mean?"

"You'll see; you will meet her soon."

"Can't wait."

"And she even got the management to allow a few dogs into the office. But we have stopped this now."

"What happened?"

"One dog was peeing all over the floor, one kept snatching people's lunches and one chewed right through the main electricity cable, so we lost power for the whole day."

"But was the dog OK?"

"It got electrocuted. Poor Jack Russell."

"I know, I know: it's such a lovely breed."

"No, no, the dog was a Great Dane."

"So who was this Jack Russell?"

"Its owner. He was so traumatised that he had to go on the CPBL."

"What's CPBL?"

"Compassionate Pet Bereavement Leave."

"They give you Compassionate Pet Bereavement Leave here?"

"They do, they do; Millie had fought very hard to get it for us, bless her. Anyway, they gave poor Jack three weeks off. It was nowhere near enough, though: he's still off work. He said his mental health had suffered irreparably. He's been in therapy ever since."

"I hope it's helping."

"Me too."

As we were getting our coffee, I spotted a notice sitting on the wall right above the sink. It said: *After the tea break, staff should empty the teapot and stand upside down on the draining board.*

"Why are you... we keeping this funny notice here, Crystal?"

Crystal giggled. "Oh, you've also noticed it's funny."

"Of course I have; how can you not?"

"Well, nobody else seems to."

"They don't?"

"Nope. Look, they don't analyse English the way we do. It's their native tongue, so they reckon they don't have to work at it. Otherwise, they would have amended this notice, wouldn't they?"

"But I thought they... we were different."

"Why?"

"Well, you know, with all these augmented reality paradigms, transcendental digital revolutions, transformational synergies and blueprints, stuff like that..."

Instead of answering, Crystal simply burst out laughing. I then remembered all the grammatical, spelling and punctuation mistakes on their... on our application form and couldn't help being overcome by sadness. Then again, however severe my limitations vis-à-vis the aforementioned augmented reality paradigms, transcendental digital revolutions and transformational synergies and blueprints – and things – I could at least help my office colleagues out with their writing and perked up a bit. At this point, Dali burst into the kitchenette.

"Aston says where is his blinkin' coffee, like."

"Sorry, sorry, Dali; Crystal was just telling me what was what."

"Did she tell ya 'bout me ship fyngy, like?"

"*What* ship thingy?"

"This aper... apre..."

"Apprenticeship," said Crystal helpfully. "Not yet. But I'm about to. You see, Shodra, we offer our young people who... who, shall we say, are less... less academically inclined a range of apprenticeships. You know what Fata always says?"

"What does she always say?"

"We at FART strongly believe that university isn't the only key to unleashing human potential."

"Well, that's true, isn't it?"

"It certainly is. But the way she says it…"

Paying little attention to Crystal, Dali seemed keen to enlarge on her career aspirations.

"And when I'm finished, like, I will be like me pookie."

"*What* pookie?"

"Chard. Our brand amba… amba…"

"Ambassador," said Crystal – just as helpfully as before. "She is also called Director of First Impressions, ha, ha, ha!"

"Well, she certainly made an impression on me, Crystal. That's largely why I'm here."

Dali nodded vigorously. "Chard said it were Gucci 'ere: you could work from 'ome, like. And bounce on space 'oppers. And get free crisps and stuff. She, like, said I would like it 'ere."

"She did? That's good. I mean hella good." I was glad I had remembered Chardonnay's instruction. "And when you have completed your apprenticeship, you should be able to progress: you may get a good job, I mean hella good, earn decent money and buy a house – things like that."

Dali looked at me in puzzlement. "*Buy* an 'ouse, like?"

"Well, that's what people do, isn't it?"

"It ain't; not in me family, like. They just give you an 'ouse, innit?"

"They do?"

"Defo. So we don' 'ave to buy an 'ouse, innit? You 'ave to pay for an 'ouse."

"Well, yes: if you are in work, you have to pay your way, Dali."

"That's why me folk, they ain't in work, like. None of 'em."

"But *you* are."

"That's why they, like, call me tanga, innit?"

"*Tanga?*"

"Bozo, like."

"*Bozo?*"

"She means stupid, Shorda." Crystal was, clearly, well versed in the parlance of our youngsters.

"Oh, I see. But I think it's brilliant that you are in work, Dali."

"Dunno. They say that, if you're in work, they don' give you nuffink. And Nana says they take stuff off you, like. But they don' take nuffink off us. And they give us an 'ouse and stuff. Proper sick!"

"I'm so sorry, Dali."

"*Why?*"

"That your relatives are sick. It's only right that the sick should be supported. Britain is very good like this. I do hope your folk will get better soon."

"*They* are *not* sick. *It* is sick, like."

"*What* is?"

"That they don' take nuffink off us, like. And give us an 'ouse and stuff."

"She means great, brilliant, things like that, Zhorda. That's what youngsters say these days," interjected the still giggling Crystal to plug another obvious gap in my education.

"Sorry, Dali; I'm glad your relatives aren't sick."

"Me too; sick! Me bruvvers, they are into all sorts, like: weightliftin', skateboardin', wrestin', bikin', rugby, stuff like that."

"That's nice, Dali. How many brothers have you got?"

"Five. They are me 'alf bruvvers, but they smack."

"Well, that's not very nice Dali; I hope they don't smack you too hard."

"No, no, *they smack*, like!"

"She means they are great." It was obvious that Crystal was finding our confabulation rather entertaining.

"Me sisters are also sporty, like: they are mad 'bout footie. And Term is into boxin'."

"Who's Term?"

"Terminator."

"Who's Terminator?"

"The new dude who's just moved in with me mum, like. He's 'eavy weight: roughs them up proper, like."

"Well, your folk do seem to be in fine fettle, Dali."

"They are, innit? Flippin' 'eck, Aston's blinkin' coffee!" Clutching a large mug containing his beverage, Dali sprinted for the door.

"How do you know all these slang words, Crystal?"

"Well, I've worked here for a while, and we have quite a few youngsters – all these Zedders. And Millennials as well. You just pick stuff up. You will do too; don't worry."

"To be honest, Crystal, the main thing I worry about is all this AI stuff. I know very little about it."

"Join the club," roared Crystal. "The only one who is

supposed to be an AI expert here is Rushdi. But Theo is also a bit of a techie; he is from Singapore."

"I didn't know that Theo was a Singaporean name."

"It isn't. Apparently, his real name is Xiao, but he changed it when he came to Britain. Anyway, he has an English surname: his grandfather was English."

"So what's his full name?"

"Theo Retic."

"Nice and easy. Actually, I might take a leaf out of his book: Szczodra is such a tongue-twister."

"I agree."

"But, Crystal, how come we are supposed to deliver this revolutionary AI transformation and everything when the rest of us know next to nothing about AI?"

"Because we know about education. And the government wants to abolish teachers – eventually."

"*To abolish teachers?*"

"Absolutely. Do you know how large our national debt is?"

"Not exactly, but I do know that it's enormous."

"Over two trillion pounds. And counting. Just servicing it costs more than our entire defence budget."

"Good grief!"

"And teachers are expensive. Besides, the youngsters are forever glued to their phones, so the government reckons that, once we've trained this AI, it could do all the teaching and assessing remotely. So we wouldn't need any teachers. Think about what a colossal saving this would be."

"Jeepers! Who cooked this up: the Tories?"

"Yep. But our current government is desperate. If they don't find more dosh somewhere – or trim their expenditure – Rachel Reeves might have to increase our taxes, and people don't like paying taxes. That's why we have all those tax avoiders. Particularly among the rich. So the scheme stays in place."

"Crafty buggers! But what do the teachers have to say about this?"

"The teachers have absolutely no idea: this stuff is top secret. I mean it's not exactly a secret *here*, although we are not supposed to talk about it openly. But we have to keep shtum until the government is ready to announce this groundbreaking initiative, ha, ha, ha!"

"They had better hire good lawyers."

"They've already started. We are also hiring: our legal department will soon be the largest one here."

"Will it really?"

"Absolutely. Bona has been very proactive."

"Who's Bona?"

"Bona Fide. Mrs. She is the Director of our Legal Department. But you won't believe the hoo-ha around *her* appointment: there was blood on the carpet."

My ears pricked up. Look, I have already confessed to my congenital curiosity when it comes to other people's affairs, haven't I? Particularly when there's blood on the carpet.

"Oh, yes?"

"Yep. There was this other candidate – Dr Culpa."

"So what happened?"

"This Dr Culpa – her full name was Dr Mea-Maxima Culpa – apparently, she had it all: Eton, Oxford, Harvard, PhDs all over the place."

"And?"

"She had applied to head our Legal Department."

"*Ours?* Why would she have wanted to work *here*... I mean, you know... I didn't mean..."

"Don't worry, don't worry; I know *exactly* what you mean." Crystal's reassurance was offered with her, by now familiar, chuckle. "I don't know, but she didn't get the job anyway. So she sued for unfair discrimination."

"And then? What happened?"

"We settled out of court. For an undisclosed sum. Obviously, we had to hire lawyers: we had no Legal Department then."

"But why would they... I mean why would we overlook such a well-qualified candidate? This Fide woman – she has no doctorate, or has she?"

"She hasn't. But she has something Dr Culpa didn't."

"Oh, yes?"

"Well, you know, there's been this rumour going around..."

Now, I defy you to remain uninterested whenever there is a rumour going around.

"Yes, yes, *yes?*"

"There is this rumour going around that she is Theo's bit on the side."

"*Theo's?* But I thought... I thought that these Asian people were very hot on family. Much more so than we are in the West."

"No, no, it's not *our* Theo – it's Theo Morphic."

"Who's Theo Morphic?"

"Our Foremost Authoritarian."

"We have *Foremost Authoritarian?*"

"Obviously. Each organisation has to have a big cheese at the top."

"But I thought it was Nota."

"No, no, she is only an Enthuser – Foremost Enthuser."

"Only?"

"I know, I know. But, you know, they are also saying—"

"What, *what* are they also saying?"

"That she is another one of Theo's bits on the side."

"Good grief: how does he find the energy?"

"Well, he is hardly ever here. Nobody has seen him for… for what – six, seven months now? Apart from Bona and Nota, obviously."

"But why… how is this allowed?"

"Well, who is to object, exactly? He is the boss. Besides, we are all allowed to work from home two days a week, so he is bound to get a far more generous allowance."

"You mean like coming into the office twice a year?"

"You are not just a pretty face."

"But what about all these Advisers: where exactly do *we* come in?"

"We are supposed to harvest tons of stuff to feed to the bots."

"Feed? How?"

"I mean train. You know you have to train the bots?"

"Y-e-e-e-s, well, I've heard something along these lines. But it sounds rather complicated."

"It is, but we don't have to worry about the actual AI training bit."

"We don't?"

"Nope. What *we* need to do is to trawl through school and college curricula, exams, monitoring mechanisms, feedback loops – stuff like that – from all four nations of the UK. Then we will just give it to the AI whizzes so that they can put it on the bots' menu. That's why we have to have a background in education. You've worked in education, I take it?"

"I have, I have, Crystal: teaching, assessment, curricula, exams – the lot."

"Me too. So we don't have to worry about the AI bit. But things can still go wrong."

"How?"

"Theo – *our* Theo – said that AI models are prone to exacerbating human bias."

"How dreadful! But how exactly?"

"He said something about data distribution shifts."

"Y-e-e-e-s?"

"It's when a diagnostic model makes mistakes because it's trained on the wrong stuff."

"That's awful!"

"Yep. He also said that AI could hallucinate."

"Good Lord!"

"Actually, I'm not sure if these two things are the same, but Theo said that we must select and organise all the data carefully before the stuff can be fed to the bot."

"So, actually, our job is quite complicated."

"Why do you think they have made us Advisers, Shodra?"

"Hmm, I imagine they thought we are the right people to do the donkey work. With all the highfalutin stuff I told them during my job interview—"

"Exactly. And before we give all this material to Theo & Co, we will have to codify, classify and arrange it."

"*All* of it? Goodness me!"

"I know, I know. And, for every single item of data we

cull, we will have to write a comprehensive report on why and how we have selected it."

"But why?"

"Because, if we get things wrong, we might even cause a complete model collapse. That's what Theo said."

"Perish the thought!" I was now seriously concerned. "Thank goodness we have this Bona. Even if she has no PhD."

"Yep, it is rather reassuring." Before I decided what to make of Crystal's chuckle, she continued with her elucidation. "Anyway, we have to document and justify everything, so that, if things do get pear-shaped, we can hide behind the process. Thankfully, we've got our garbled website; I take it you've seen it?" Crystal's chuckle had now metamorphosed into full-throated laughter.

"Obviously! I had to memorise the stuff for my job interview."

"Yep, it's utter gobbledygook, but this is precisely why it's so helpful."

"*Helpful? How?*"

"If the worst comes to the worst, we can always turn around, shrug our shoulders and insist that we have followed all the processes listed on the website to the letter, so whatever has gone wrong couldn't *possibly* be our fault."

"But what if this is challenged?"

"It can't be challenged."

"Why?"

"Because it's meaningless: nobody understands it – including us. So how could you marshal a cogent argument against something that is unintelligible? And, if people think that this stuff actually means something, they may worry that it's only they who don't understand it. Nobody likes to seem ignorant, do they?"

"No, I suppose they don't. Actually, I'm still having flashbacks. And the occasional full-length nightmare. I mean, about having to memorise all the stuff for my job interview."

"Don't worry: if they get too bad, you can always refer yourself to our Wellness Department, ha, ha, ha!"

"We actually have a Wellness *Department?* I thought we outsourced the running of all these wellness programmes."

"Some we do outsource, but our Wellness Department is also very active. Not that I've had any dealings with them, but colleagues say that Molly Coddle and Val Erian are excellent. They reckon another year in therapy and Jack should be well enough to return to work – albeit on a part-time basis."

"The one with the electrocuted dog?"

"Actually, the one without it."

"Yes, yes, of course; poor doggie."

"Molly and Val send us these bulletins with all sorts of weird and wonderful articles offering all kinds of advice on health, welfare and work-life balance."

"Isn't this good, Crystal?"

"See for yourself. I've got the most recent issue on my phone."

Having done some scrolling, Crystal located the bulletin in question and passed her phone over to me. The publication, bearing a tastefully designed logo with Well-Beings at its centre, was entitled *Always look on the bright side of life* and read as follows:

> 'According to research, optimists have better physical and mental health, greater success, more satisfying relationships, better coping skills and live longer than do profits of doom.'

"Oh, Crystal: '*profits* of doom'!"

Crystal was also laughing.

"If you are a prophet, you are bound to make a profit: just tell people what the future holds, and they will give you money, ha, ha, ha! You'd better get used to imaginative spelling: you'll see lots of it here."

"Uhm, I've noticed, Crystal. I just hope we can apply the same imagination to all this AI wizardry. What does Rushdi think about it? With all its biases, hallucinations, model collapses and things?"

"I haven't the foggiest."

"O-o-o-o?"

"Nobody does."

"How come?"

"Because Rushdi works from home, and we hardly ever see him. Once a month – if we are lucky."

"But… but don't we all have to be in the office three days a week?"

"*We* do, yes – but not Rushdi."

"How come?"

"Because he doesn't like getting up in the morning."

"Well, who does? But we still have to do it."

"Not if we are Rushdi, we don't."

"I'm not with you."

"Look, he is of a different ethnic origin."

"Yes. So?"

"He said that having to get up in the morning would seriously damage his mental health."

"Did he now? So why didn't they... we just sack him?"

"*Sack him?* Can you imagine the adverse publicity if this got out? We might be accused of racism, bias, prejudice, bigotry, inequity, exclusion – all sorts. And then this might be widely reported. You know the British press. And all the social media. Besides, he is the only AI whizz we've got."

At this point, the door opened and Dali burst in, accompanied by a slightly older female with a deepest frown I had ever seen on a human being, which made her look rather fierce. A Millennial, I guessed.

"This is Millie, like," announced Dali before refilling the kettle and switching it on. "Aston, like, fancies another cuppa."

"Pleased to meet you, Millie; I'm Szczodra. Crystal has told me lots of nice things about you."

"*Nice?*" For some reason, Millie didn't seem too pleased. "My job is *not* to be nice – my job is *to fight*."

"Yes, yes, of course; Crystal did say that you were an excellent fighter." To change the tricky subject, I quickly turned to Dali with a feigned interest in her thirst-quenching mission. "Does Aston always drink black coffee?"

"Trigger, trigger!" shouted Millie.

I was slightly baffled. "I've seen no guns here, Millie; don't worry."

"You are triggering me, Zharda, you are triggering me!"

"*How?*"

"In this day and age, you can't say 'black'!"
"But it's coffee."
"All the same. It's been banned."
"What? *Coffee?*"
"No, saying 'black'."

To her credit, Dali gave Millie a dubious look. "But, when Term smashes them other dudes up, like, he says they black out. And me mum, like, she says you can get cheapo ciggies on the black market. And I got lotsa them bargins on Black Friday. Amazon, they would know, innit?"

The girl certainly had a point there. But Millie would have none of it. "We pride ourselves on being colour-blind!"

"But Chardonnay said you... we prided ourselves on delivering customer focus, Millie."

Appearing irritated, Millie was about to say something, but Dali got there first. "When you're, like, colour-blind, you can't see no colour, innit? But I can see lotsa them colours, like."

I have to say I was beginning to revise my opinion about the girl. Probably as sharp as a tack. You see, you must never jump to conclusions.

"In this day and age, we have to be extremely vigilant – we have to watch what we say. All the time. After all, we are an equal, opportune, diverse and inclusive organisation," continued Millie. She then addressed me directly: "Haven't you seen our Equalities, Opportunities, Diversity and Inclusion Policies?"

"I have, I have, Millie. Actually, I was struck by how equal and opportune you... we were. So what..."

At this point, Crystal covered her mouth and turned away from us rather abruptly, her shoulders heaving spasmodically. She couldn't have been laughing, could she?

"So what can we say instead, Millie?"

Millie creased her already furrowed brow, pondered my question for a brief moment and said: "Charcoal would be best."

"All right then: get Aston some charcoal coffee, Dali."

"But Nana, like, uses charcoal for heatin'; Aston wouldn't like it in his coffee, like."

What did I say? Sharp as a tack.

"OK, just get him coffee without milk. And tell him we won't be a minute."

After Dali and Millie left, Crystal was still laughing – although no longer surreptitiously.

"Well, this Dali isn't stupid, you know, Crystal."

"I know, I know; she is actually quite bright. Her background works against her, but we might be able to make something of her here."

"I do hope so."

"Actually, Aston has entered her for the General Certificate in Administrative Capacities for Digital Horizons."

"Has he really?" I was beginning to see the man in a new light. What have I told you about never jumping to conclusions?

"Yep. But she doesn't know about it. We didn't want to spook her: there is obviously no history of education in her family. So we will be assessing her covertly. And, if she passes, it will come as a nice surprise, won't it?"

"What a lovely idea!" I must say that, even though I

harboured certain doubts as to whether horizons could have capacities – administrative or otherwise – I was beginning to warm to our organisation.

"What did you use to teach, Crystal?"

"French. You?"

"English as a Foreign Language. But that was in Poland. Before the Berlin Wall came down. We were in the clutches of the Soviet Union – God, how we hated them – but we valued education. Everybody in Warsaw wanted to learn English."

"I'm not surprised: it's the lingua franca the world over."

"The Brits don't know how lucky they are to have English as their native tongue. I'm completely mad about English, Crystal. What a magnificent language: so rich, so expressive, so nuanced, so flexible, so… so fabulous!"

"Yep, I agree, Shodra."

"And its grammar – it's absolutely fascinating, don't you think?"

"Yep; shame it was off the menu in Britain for such a long time."

"Dreadful shame, Crystal. But my Polish students were very keen to learn English grammar."

"Lucky you. Mine here in England were expecting me to turn cartwheels. And the discipline…" Crystal shook her head.

"Well, at least you are out of it now, Crystal."

"Out of the frying pan and into the fire, ha, ha, ha!"

"What do you mean?"

"You'll see, you'll see."

"You are beginning to worry me now, Crystal."

"Look, you've survived communism – you'll survive FART!"

4

Bombshells and Revelations

When Crystal and I returned to the office, I could see that there were a few new faces there.

But, before I was able to conduct a brief inspection, Aston turned to us and said: "We are supposed to do some work here, ladies; you know what I'm saying; you've been gone ages. I've had two coffees in that space. And am ready for a third, actually. Now, let's—"

"No, no, you can't say this, Aston."

This came from Millie, who must have heard Aston's admonishment.

"What, we can't say that they expect us to do some work here?"

"No, no, Aston, we no longer say 'ladies.'"

"So *what* do we say? Women?"

"No, no, no! We definitely cannot say 'women'!"

"*Why not?*"

"Because it's discriminatory."

Now, this was truly electrifying: the entire floor stopped

what it was doing and was now looking at Millie. With a smirk, Aston pretended to be seeking enlightenment.

"So what do you reckon we should be using instead, Millie?"

"People with cervixes."

Ready to join in the game, I feigned alarm. "But, Millie, I have no cervix."

"So you identify as a person of my gender?"

"I don't *identify* as a person of your gender, Millie – I *am* a person of your gender. And sex."

"But all people of our sex have cervixes."

"Well, young people like you may have, but, at my age, some of us will have had hysterectomies. And, if it's a total hysterectomy, they take your cervix out."

"Total bollocks!" boomed Aston. "Cut it out!" Regrettably, this instructional interlude failed to quell his annoyance with Crystal and me because he gave us an irritated look and barked: "We've got a lot of stuff to get through, right? And Zodra needs all this training, you know what I'm saying." This made me rather anxious: was I rocking the boat before I even managed to clamber aboard?

"Awfully, awfully sorry, Aston, but… but… Crystal was… I mean I was… I mean it was very educational: I've learnt a lot about your… our organisation."

This didn't seem to appease Aston. "Remember, you are supposed to learn from *me*, right?" He paused for a brief moment, and, when he restarted, his tone seemed somewhat graver: "I've got an STD, you know what I'm saying."

At this precise moment, I heard a strange gurgling noise emanating from my immediate right, where Crystal's desk was. When I turned around, I could see that my new friend had buried her head in her hands and was shaking uncontrollably. My goodness, was she *so* profoundly affected by Aston's shocking confession? Mind you, I was startled as well. But, surely, if Aston was brave enough to open up about such a personal and sensitive thing, he deserved our sympathy and support.

"So brave of you, Aston, so very brave."

"*Brave?* I wouldn't say so. But it certainly wasn't easy, you know what I'm saying."

"I'm sure it wasn't, I'm sure it wasn't."

"Not many people have it, right?"

I wondered if he had made this observation because, in fact, he needed to be reassured of the exact opposite. Some people resort to similar strategies, you know.

"W-e-e-e-ll, maybe not many *young* people – not these days, Aston. But I've heard that it's a rather different story with the older generation."

"Bollocks, you've heard wrong, right?" Aston sounded even more annoyed than before, so I must have made the wrong deduction. In any case, I knew I had to be as conciliatory as possible.

"W-e-e-e-ll, maybe I have, maybe I have. But, whether I'm right or wrong, I hope you are not too worried. These days, they can—"

"*Worried?* Why should I be *worried?*"

"No, no, you *shouldn't* be worried. Because, you know… it's… it's… it can be…be very effective, this—"

"It *is* very effective."

"Yes, thank goodness for antibiotics."

"*Antibiotics? What are you on about, Zarda?*"

"Well, if one... if one has... has a... a sexually transmitted disease—"

"*A sexually transmitted disease? Who* has a sexually transmitted disease?"

"What do you mean *who*? *You*. You... you said you had an STD."

At this precise moment, Crystal sprung up from her chair and bolted for the door. I never thought that the woman could run so quickly. At her age.

"Honestly, Surda: I meant my *Studies in Transactionality Diploma*."

"O-o-o-o-o, I s-e-e-e-e, silly me!" I must say I was rather relieved, but I also felt quite sheepish.

"Haven't you heard of this diploma?"

"Can't say I have, Aston. Do you have to study transactionality?"

"Absolutely, absolutely! Basically, *all* employment is transactional, right? So you have to study transactionality."

"You do?"

"Absolutely. Look at Trump: he is all about transactionality. You give me this, and I'll give you that. Or, rather, I won't clobber you as hard as I had threatened. This must be why they elected him president again."

"It must?"

"Absolutely. And, in employment, they give you money and perks, and you give them your labour. The more money and perks they give you, the more labour you give them, you know what I'm saying."

"Not necessarily."

"Not necessarily? What do you mean *not necessarily?*"

"Well, look at those poor people working at Amazon

fulfilment centres. Or cleaners and domestics, checkout operators, poultry dressers, care workers, delivery drivers... They don't get much money or many perks, yet they work really hard."

"Exactly!"

"Exactly *what?*"

"They can't have studied transactionality, can they? Not to a diploma level, anyway."

"Maybe not, maybe not." I was acutely aware of the imperative to humour Aston. "Does your diploma cover intrinsic rewards?"

"*Intrinsic* rewards?"

"Well, yes, if you love your job—"

"*Love your job?*" Aston looked stunned.

"Yes. If you love your job, perhaps you don't have to be quite so transactional. Because it carries intrinsic rewards."

"Such as?"

"A sense of purpose and meaning, pride in your accomplishments and creativity, self-fulfilment, satisfaction, autonomy, intellectual stimulation—"

"Intellectual stimulation from stuff like *transformational synergies and blueprints?*"

"I didn't mean necessarily—"

"Nah, forget it. You just angle for as much as you can get and then haggle at every step. And the more they give you, the more they value you, right?"

"They *do?*" Having myself done no haggling at all, I had no experience in this arena. But I was again overcome by sadness: this must be why I had never had a fancy title. Or the dosh that goes with it. Why do you think I was still working at my age?

"Absolutely, Shodra. Basically, if you are paying good money to a dunce, what does this make *you*? So they convince themselves that you are an Einstein, right?"

"They *do*?"

"Absolutely. As I've said, you'll need a lot of training, you know what I'm saying. But let me introduce you to other colleagues." With this, Aston turned around and pointed towards one of the new faces – this one encircled by a bird's nest of frizzy hair. "Sharda, this is our Mala. Mala Prop. Mala, meet Zhorda."

I was relieved that Aston's homily on transactionality had come to an end. "Lovely to meet you, Mala; how are you?"

"Yea, I'm good, I'm good."

Now, if you were me, would *you* be able to resist the temptation of a brief linguistic intervention? I certainly couldn't.

"I don't doubt that you are good, Mala – I'm sure you are *very* good – but how *are* you?"

"Yea, yea, I'm doing good."

"That's excellent, Mala: one can do very well by doing good. So you must be doing *well*."

"Uh? Rewind."

"Sorry, Mala, it was just… I was just… I have a thing about the English language, you know."

"No bother, Sharda, we totally get it: English can be murder to foreign people. Aston had warned us about you."

"Did he really?"

"Yea, he said you were Polish. But your English isn't *that* bad. You'll get there – eventually." The sympathetic tone in Mala's voice made it abundantly clear that she had failed to grasp my linguistic point.

"I hope so, Mala, I hope so. Actually, some people say that I am excessively Polish."

"Ha, ha, ha, I'm liking it, very good. For a Pole. There's a lot of Polish ex-patriots here."

"Oh dear, that's terrible."

"Uh? *Why?*"

"To turn your back on your motherland like that. Maybe they have retained at least *some* loyalty to—"

"Uh? Rewind."

"She means *expatriates*." This exegesis was whispered by Crystal, who had returned from wherever she had earlier fled to.

"I know, I know," I whispered back.

Thankfully, Mala didn't catch my remark, her eyebrows surging towards each other in a determined attempt to link up. "That's *exactly* what I said."

"I'm terribly sorry, Mala; it must be my English."

"No bother; we totally get it. You'll get there – eventually."

I had to make a supreme effort to keep a straight face, but the occasion undoubtedly demanded physiognomic discipline. Thankfully, Aston now turned towards another new face, which belonged to a red-haired gentleman in a tartan jacket. Actually, the face seemed vaguely familiar, although I couldn't quite put my finger on it.

"Shorda, this is Jock; he's only just joined us. Jock is from Glasgow. He had something to do with the Scottish Curriculum for Excellence."

So *that* is where I met him! I didn't really know him because we worked in different departments, but our paths have definitely crossed. And I couldn't help remembering his name – could *you?* It was Jock Strap.

"Yes, yes, I have met Jock: we worked for the same organisation in Scotland. Hello, Jock; not sure if you remember me: I'm Szczodra. Long time no see."

"Upty?"

"I… I beg your pardon, Jock?"

"Happenin'?"

"Uhmm… sorry?"

"Whit's yer chat?"

"Uhmm… y-e-e-e-s…"

"Yer lookin' a bit peely wally."

"Uhmm… yes, yes… of course, of course…"

Now, I don't know what strategy you *yourself* adopt when you cannot comprehend what your interlocutor is saying. I find it rather embarrassing to keep asking them to repeat themselves so, after unsuccessfully petitioning for a translation a couple of times, I tend to agree, perhaps a tad too enthusiastically, with whatever comes out of their mouths while praying that I am not answering a question asking me if I think they are stupid. Anyway, that was my stratagem in Scotland, although I have to say that I was working alongside well-educated professionals whose accent was, by and large, intelligible – *even* to me. With one exception. Like Jock, Duncan was a Glaswegian, and understanding what he was saying was a sheer impossibility. I mean, would *you* be able to comprehend the likes of: 'I hae ma doots', 'Bolt ya rocket', 'Gonnae no' dae that', 'You're a pure sook', 'Naw ye wurny', 'Ah dinnae ken', 'Yae cannae dae it' – stuff like this? Actually, these particular utterances were subsequently translated for me by my Scottish colleagues, who appeared sympathetic to my plight. But countless others remained an enigma.

Did a similar fate await me at FART? The omens weren't good. But I couldn't dwell on such a perturbing prospect for too long because I was still facing Jock, who was now saying, "Aye, aye." Well, at least I knew what *that* meant, so it was something, I suppose. Feigning a delight at having been reunited with a long-lost friend, I was nevertheless anxious to bring our one-sided preliminaries to a close.

"Lovely to see you again, Jock. I'm sure we'll…"

Before I was able to proceed, however, I was distracted by Dali, who was waving a phone receiver at Aston and saying, rather loudly, "Aston, she ain't gonna go away, like."

"Who?"

"One of Nota's whatsits… emsies or somynk."

"You mean Management Consultants, Dali?"

"Them ones, them ones!"

"Oh, no!" groaned Aston. "Tell them I'm up to my eyes."

"That's what I said, innit? But she, like, she says she's been callin' Nota all mumf. And emailin' 'er. She says she didn't 'ave no reply, like."

"Tell her we have *all* been up to our eyes all month."

"That's what I said, innit?"

I must say I was impressed by Dali's initiative: to attempt to repel a caller by coming up – *unprompted* – with such a convincing excuse was quite remarkable. I'm sure that the HMRC could use her talents.

The girl continued: "She ain't gonna go away, like."

Aston gave a deep sigh and conceded defeat. But, before he picked up the phone, he turned to me: "I'd better take this, Zarda. But at least you will be able to learn how we handle things here: you'll be listening in."

He then lifted the receiver, and I started listening in with great concentration, which definitely wasn't feigned: it would be really helpful to start learning how they… how *we* handled things here.

"Good morning. FART here. Aston Ishing speaking. How can I help in this space?"

Ever since I settled in this wonderful country aeons ago, I have been admiring the seemingly effortless courtesy with which the natives conduct their various transactions. In the Soviet-oppressed Poland of my youth, where everything was nationalised and where you didn't have to worry about being nice to your customers because you had no competitors, the best you could have hoped for would be a curt, "What do you want?" But here, their conversations are mesmerisingly civilised.

"Good morning. I've had this email… Ms Nota Clue emailed me…"

"What's the name, please?"

"Misty Fied. Mrs."

"As in Al-Fayed?"

"No, no: F-i-e-d."

"Thank you. When did she email you?"

"Last February."

"Last Febiuary, last Febiuary, hmmm. So what did she say?"

"I am not quite sure…"

"You are not quite sure, are you?" I could see that Aston was rather good at encouraging his interlocutors.

"No; I'm not; sorry. Perhaps you could help…"

"I need to see the email, Mrs Fied. Would you please forward it to me?"

"Of course, of course; thank you."

It didn't take long before the email landed in Aston's inbox. I could hardly contain my curiosity as I drew even closer and peered at his computer screen. The email went like this:

Dear Mrs. Fied

Having spoken to the Foremost Authoritarian, and the Director of the Highly Strategic Directorate a concensus has been made that the nature of the Overarching Management Consultancy Tasks' required for you to achieve and the time frame in which the relevent priority deliverables' are scheduled to be delivered are highly conflicting factors in securing both the consistency in the quality of the Management Consultancy Decisions' you make and in the knock on affect this may have for our carefully designed Radicalisation Programme in persuence of Key Government Priorities', Visions', Missions', Pledges', Initiatives', and Strategies'.

Regards.
Nota Clue. Cert BURP DUNG DUMB
Foremost Enthuser
Innovation Division
Transformation Department
Radicalisation Directorate
FART

I gasped, but my in-depth ponder of all the linguistic intricacies therein would have to wait, as Aston was continuing with the illuminating exchange.

"So what seems to be the problem, Mrs Fied?"

"I... I can't understand what Ms Clue was trying to say."

Aston's face expressed utter astonishment. "*You. Can't. Understand.*"

"No, I'm sorry."

Between you and me, I wasn't entirely surprised that Mrs Fied was baffled, but the reason appeared totally lost on Aston, who was nevertheless making a concerted effort not to let irritation show in his voice.

"It *does* seem rather straightforward, doesn't it, Mrs Fied?"

"Uhmm, no, it doesn't."

"*It doesn't?* Basically, Mrs Fied, it says that you are sacked, right?"

"*Where?*"

"*In the email!* And it explains *why* you are sacked!"

"Does it *really?*"

"It does indeed, Mrs Fied, it does indeed. Because you don't meet deadlines – basically. So we won't be using you at this moment in time; thank you." And with this, Aston hung up. I was beginning to admire the man: after all, he was clearly peeved, yet he managed to keep his cool throughout his exchange with Mrs Fied beautifully. That's what I mean by the innate courtesy of the natives. Class! And, of course, his ability to grasp Nota's meaning with such ease was simply astounding.

"If *that's* not clear, I don't know *what* is, you know what I'm saying."

"W-e-e-e-ll, Aston, I... I would have tried to... to polish it a little bit, to make it a bit easier to... to understand."

"*You?* With *your* English?"

"Well, you probably mean my accent, but..."

"Look here, Shurda, it took a lot of meetings, right?"

"What did?"

"Agreeing on the best form of words to let underperforming MCs know that we won't be using them again."

"Who agreed this form of words?"

"The Foremost Authoritarian, the Director of the Highly Strategic Directorate, Nota – *and me!*"

Aha-a-a-a, so that's why Aston knew *exactly* what this garbled message meant. I must say I was a bit disappointed that he should have had a hand in such an enterprise.

"I s-e-e-e. But... but, Aston, couldn't you at least have checked your message for grammar, punctuation and spelling?"

"Grammar, punctuation and spelling? We don't bother with grammar, punctuation and spelling: we are native speakers. We know what we mean."

"But... but you have... there is this... this dangling participle..."

"Dangling *what?*"

"Participle."

"Mala, have you ever heard about this dangling nonsense?"

Mala, whose desk was on the other side of Aston's, burst out laughing. "Never, ha, ha, ha!"

"But it isn't nonsense – cross my heart and hope to die."

"So what's this part-principle, then?" sniggered Mala.

"A *par-ti-ci-ple*. *Having spoken* is a participle – a verb form – and Nota has related it to *a consensus*, which is spelt with an 'S', by the way, but a consensus hasn't spoken to anybody – Nota has."

"Of course a consensus hasn't spoken to anybody; do you think I'm stupid, Shurba?"

"No, no, Aston, of course not, of course not! It's just that this is… this is what the email says."

"Bollocks!"

Although I knew I was skating on thin ice, I've told you about my obsession with English grammar, haven't I? The passion of my life and all that? So I ploughed on regardless.

"But… but it does, Aston. And these… these greengrocers' apostrophes…"

"For Pete's sake, what have greengrocers got to do with anything?"

"Well, you don't put an apostrophe at the end of *apples*, *pears*, *leeks* and such like, but, when you visit any market, you will see that greengrocers often write *apple's*, *pear's*, *leek's* – incorrectly. It's not only greengrocers who do this, of course, but that's the name given to this error. Such nouns are called regular."

"*All* words in English are regular, you know what I'm saying. You may have some irregular ones in your Polish, but everything in English is regular and proper."

"No, no, English *does* have some irregular nouns, Aston. For example, goose – geese, child – children, mouse – mice, man – men, woman – women… I mean people with cervixes," I quickly corrected myself before

Millie could intervene. "Actually, *cervix* is a regular noun but *people* is an example of an irregular plural. Unless it refers to an ethnic group. But the apostrophised nouns in Nota's email are all regular."

"That's *exactly* what I've said, Zurba."

"Which is why all these apostrophes are incorrect and should have been removed, Aston. After all, we are not greengrocers."

"Obviously we are *not!*" With this, Aston shook his head and gave Mala a knowing look, to which she reciprocated in a similar vein. Although I should have probably capitulated at that point, I couldn't resist the temptation to flaunt my linguistic expertise a bit more. This is the only thing I have which is worthy of flaunting, by the way, so, when an opportunity presents itself, I seize it with both hands.

"You also… there are also some misspellings… muddled collocations… crazy punctuation… a bit too much jargon…"

"Bollocks!" thundered Aston. "You obviously haven't had enough exposure to good English. But at least you are in the right place here, so watch, listen and learn, you know what I'm saying."

Having finally grasped the futility of my endeavour, I thought it expedient to change the subject. But, just as I was about to pose a question about how often Aston had an opportunity to engage with the Foremost Authoritarian – given that the latter worked predominantly from home – Dali's head popped up from behind Aston's in-tray.

"Aston, you're meeting them dudes from this Shared… Shared Committee, like!"

"Blast! I've nearly forgotten. Shorba, we'll do some training after I've come back; gotta shoot – laters!"

"Why are we sharing this committee, Crystal? Is there a shortage of committees here?" I asked my colleague after Aston had disappeared from view.

"On the contrary, on the contrary! We are not sharing it with anybody: it's called the Shared-*Vision* Committee."

"So who do we share this vision with?"

"No, no, I couldn't possibly spoil your fun, Shodra; wait till you get your training." She was now openly laughing, which, I have to admit, only aroused my curiosity, but I immediately spotted an opportunity to return to my favourite subject. I could see that Dew, whose desk was opposite mine, had been listening to my exchange with Aston and decided to make my move. Admittedly, the girl was very quiet, which was hardly surprising given that she can't even have been twenty, but at least she would have remembered what they had taught her at school.

"Dew, were you taught English grammar at school?"

"Yes, but I didn't understand much."

"You didn't?"

"No, and my teacher, she, like, didn't understand much either."

"*She* didn't? How do you know?"

"Because she said. She, like, said that she hadn't been taught English grammar herself. Apparently, they didn't, like, teach grammar in the seventies."

"I know, I know. But, if she didn't understand grammar, why did she teach it?"

"Because they couldn't find anyone else. But she said that it wasn't important anyway."

"Why?"

"Because we are native speakers, and we know what we mean."

"But grammar is *incredibly* important for clear communication – whether you are a native speaker or not. It's like mortar which holds linguistic bricks together so that you can convey exactly the meaning you want to convey. But communication is not just about meaning: it's also about effect."

"*Effect?*"

"Absolutely." As soon as I said this, I realised I was beginning to acquire one of Aston's mannerisms, but I suppose this was inevitable. "You want to express yourself in an appropriate *manner*."

"What do you mean?"

"Well, your language should suit your audience as well as the purpose and occasion of each utterance you make and each piece of writing you produce. And, when you write, punctuation and spelling are also important."

"Hmm," pondered the girl.

"If you like, I could teach you a bit about English grammar. And about writing in general."

"*You?* Could you really?"

"Of course. I've been steeped in English grammar for more than fifty years. It's absolutely fascinating."

"Is it really? All right, then; thank you."

Obviously, I couldn't leave Dali out and turned to the girl. "I'm going to teach Dew some English grammar; would you like to join us?"

Dali rested her chin on her hand and sucked on the end of her pen as she pondered my offer thoughtfully. This gave me an opportunity to continue.

"You see, Dali, if you want to get on at work – and in life in general – you need to express yourself well. And grammar helps you to do this. You can then progress, and people will look up to you. You and Dew are both very young, and I am sure that, with a bit of… of help, you can go far and get great jobs."

"Will they, like, give me a motor?" enquired Dali.

"Quite likely."

"And me own office, like?"

"My."

"No, not *your* office; *me own*, like."

"*My* own; we say *my* own." The highly sceptical expression on Dali's face made me quickly add: "*Me office* is fine in informal contexts – for example, among your friends – but I think you should practise saying *my*. It will help you when you are having a job interview. If you want to progress – after you have completed your apprenticeship – you will have lots of job interviews, you know."

The girl nodded her head. "And will they, like, let me work from 'ome?"

"Probably. When you are in a senior position, you can do what you like – more or less. Look at our Foremost Authoritarian: apparently, he is hardly ever in the office."

"Sick," declared Dali.

Delighted to have succeeded in recruiting not only Dew but also Dali, I knew I had to strike while the iron…I mean while Aston was out of the office.

"Shall we start with fillers?"

"Best not, like." Dali looked at me sceptically again.

"Why not? We all use fillers."

"No, we don,'" retorted the girl. "Me... my influenza..."

"Oh, dear, you've got influenza? I'm so sorry, Dali."

"No, no: me... my influenza off TikTok, like. She says not to mess with fillers; you can, like, get a trout pout if they give you too much filler in your lips, innit?"

"Oh, you mean your *influencer!*"

The girl nodded. "That's what I said, innit?"

Realising I couldn't address all the relevant grammatical points all at once, I decided to concentrate on the fillers.

"I didn't mean *injectable* fillers, Dali. The fillers I meant are used in speech. They are called 'empty words' because they mark pauses or hesitation."

"Could you give us an example?" requested Dew.

"I was just about to. *Oh, mm, umm, huh, like, you know, I mean, actually, basically* are all fillers."

"I see," said Dew.

"And there is one filler which you use all the time."

"Which one?"

"*Like.*"

Both girls nodded in unison, with Dew reinforcing their general agreement with my assertion thus: "Everyone, like, uses it all the time."

"Well, yes, I know, I know; it's very common among young people. But older people don't use it quite as much. And, when you are having your job interview, you will be interviewed by older people. So it would be best if you perhaps... perhaps tried to use it less often."

Both girls looked at me quizzically, and Dali asked: "Will they, like, give me the job if I, like, use it less often?"

"Well, they will be looking for other things as well, but it will help. So maybe you could think about it and start trying not to use it quite so much – especially in formal situations."

I could see both girls thinking deeply about what I had just said. But it didn't take long before Dali cocked her head to one side and enquired: "Is *well* also a filler, like? I mean is *well* a filler? You use it all the time."

I was hugely impressed: with a bit of assistance, the girl will go far, no two ways about it.

"Yes, Dali, it certainly is."

"But is it a *good* filler?"

"What do you mean 'a good filler'? Fillers are neither good nor bad; it's just something we all use."

"But you've just said that *like* was a bad filler, like."

"We-e-e-ell, not exactly, not in *informal* situations."

"But is *well* better?"

I must admit that I found myself momentarily lost for words. "Uhm… well… I mean… I mean people, older people… I mean if you are applying for jobs… or have to speak to senior people or to important customers or have a radio interview or… or things like that… the filler *well* wouldn't stand out quite so much." Then, having regained my composure, I added: "In fact, like is not used *at all* in the public life and the media. Do you listen to the BBC?"

"Defo," answered Dali without any hesitation.

"That's excellent. So you know you won't hear people using the filler *like* there, don't you?"

"But, like, I do! I mean I do. Bear is usin' it all the time."

"Who's Bear?"

"Me other… my other influenza, erm, influencer."

"And what programme does this influencer present?"

"Bear's Buzzing Content. On TikTok."

"Oh, I s-e-e-e, so that's what you meant by the BBC."

"Bet," agreed the girl.

"Well, I meant the British Broadcasting Corporation. Have you heard about it?"

The girl shook her head.

"They do lots of radio and television programmes. And the people presenting them are paid a lot of money."

"Gucci."

"But they don't use *like* as a filler. Because it's a formal context – usually. If you get the chance, perhaps you could give TikTok a rest and listen to the BBC. I mean the British Broadcasting Corporation."

Dali nodded her head. And, Bear's Buzzing Content notwithstanding, I knew I was in: both young ladies were definitely worth investing in, and I was going to help them as much as I could.

"But, you see, writing is even harder."

"Why?" enquired Dew.

"Because you also have to think about spelling and punctuation. And Nota's… their email was all mangled. They can't even have spellchecked it."

"But they say that spellchecker sometimes gets things wrong," interjected Dew.

"And they are right. But that's why you would also use a dictionary."

"*A dictionary?* We've never used a dictionary."

"Not even at school?"

"No, we are native speakers."

"All the same, you should. You can find many interesting words in a dictionary. I've got lots of dictionaries at home; I could bring one to the office for you if you like."

"Sick!"

"And I could also bring a thesaurus."

"A toy size?" enquired Dew.

"No, no, a normal size."

The girl looked puzzled. "But… but you can't."

"Why not? I have lots."

"But… but they got extinct."

"Books don't get extinct."

"I don't mean books – I mean *dinosaurs!*"

"No, no, no: a thesaurus is *not* a dinosaur, Dew." I have to say that I almost burst out laughing but manged to stop myself in time. The girls needed to be reassured that I was on their side.

5

Ploys, Schemes and Strategies

"We are going to Nairn," announced Aston upon his return.

"*Nairn?* Great!"

"If I were you, I wouldn't get too excited."

"But I've always wanted to go to Nairn, Aston."

"Now is your chance."

"But it will take us a while."

"Nah. You use an escalator, right?"

"*But you can't get to Nairn on an escalator!*"

"Not if it's broken, no. But they have just repaired it."

"But, Aston, I don't understand: Nairn is in the north of Scotland."

"Nah, Nairn is on the twenty-fifth floor."

"*What?*"

"Nairn is one of our meeting rooms, right? Basically, all our meeting rooms have names. Didn't Crystal explain? You said she'd been telling you about FART. In the kitchenette."

"No, Aston, she didn't."

Aston shook his head. "Gossip, gossip, gossip: you are gone ages, and she doesn't even tell you about our meeting rooms."

"It must have slipped her mind, Aston; I'm sure she had intended to."

"Basically, Sharda, all our meeting rooms have names: Nairn, Dundee, Perth, Stirling, Dumfries…"

"But, Aston, they are all Scottish."

"Of course they are. You know the Scottish Independence Referendum?"

"Obviously. In 2014."

"So you know that the British government was looking for ways to persuade the Scots to vote to remain."

"Yes, yes, unsurprisingly. Erecting trade barriers with your closest and largest trading partner isn't too clever, is it? Look at Brexit."

"Too right, it isn't."

"But what has the Scottish referendum got to do with our meeting rooms, Aston?"

"Everything, everything, you know what I'm saying."

"In what way?"

"Basically, the British government decided that England needed to do all it possibly could to show that it treasured Scotland beyond measure, right? And what better way than giving your meeting rooms Scottish names?"

"I s-e-e-e-e. But, as far as I can tell, Scotland doesn't use English meeting rooms, so how would it know?"

"Basically, intelligence, espionage, penetration, moles, plants, things like that. They could easily infiltrate our organisations: we have no ID cards in this country, you know what I'm saying."

"Hmm, do you think this Jock – could he possibly be…?" Obviously, I hushed my tone as I was saying this, making sure that my long-lost Glaswegian associate didn't catch my remark.

"He might be, he might be, Shorda; he's been very quiet."

I can't say I was surprised, what with Jock being the possessor of an impenetrable accent and indecipherable lexicon.

"Anyways, they haven't seceded yet, so we are still on the same side – just. As long as he tells his countrymen how much we adore them, huh, huh, huh! Let's go, Zarda."

I followed Aston out of the office. The lift had, indeed, been brought back to life, and we reached Nairn in no time. The room was fairly small but welcoming: there was a large plate of biscuits on the table – four varieties – with a coffee machine in one corner and a water cooler in another. There wasn't much of a view, the room facing a peeling grey facade of the building opposite, which was even higher than ours, but you don't expect views in meeting rooms, do you? Getting stuck right into the biscuits, Aston nevertheless did not seem to want to look as if he was trying to monopolise them.

"Have a biscuit, Shorda. Basically, we have to last till lunch, right? The chocolate digestives are the best."

Having polished off all the chocolate digestives and well over half of the chocolate chip ones, Aston turned to me with a solemn look.

"First things first. Do you know what we as an organisation are about?"

Mightily relieved that I had conducted a thorough

website research for my job interview, I volunteered the memorised bumf with a feeling approximating confidence while being mindful of the need to handle Aston with a certain degree of caution.

"Well, we are obviously about championing the embedding and enhancing of transformational synergies and capacities…"

"Blueprints… synergies and *blueprints*, right?"

"Of course, of course, Aston – synergies and *blueprints*. We are also about unleashing revolutionary… revolutionary transition strategy…"

"Revolutionary *digital radicalisation*, right?"

"Of course, of course, Aston. And pursuing digital paradigms, schemes and… and strategies for… for the unparalleled dominance on the world stage."

"*Unassailable* dominance, right? And also *blueprints.*"

"Of course, of course, and also blueprints. *Unassailable* blueprints."

"Nah, unassailable *dominance*, right?"

"Of course, of course – silly me!"

Aston gave me a penetrating look and emitted a deep sigh. "You've got a lot to learn, you know what I'm saying. Anyways, all our activities – our wide-ranging activities – serve an overarching purpose; is our overarching purpose on your radar?"

"Uhm, emm… to… to revolutionise the society's… society's covenant framework for… for national renewal?"

"Nah."

"Uhm, to… to… penetrate the governmental… the governmental growth and productivity agenda?"

"Nah."

I have to admit that I was getting rather desperate. "To… to transcend… transcend the horizon… the horizon…" At that point, I got well and truly stuck.

"Nah. Our overarching purpose is to stay in business. To keep our jobs, you know what I'm saying."

"*To keep our jobs?*"

"Absolutely. We are in a very precarious position, right?"

"We are, Aston? *Really?*"

"Absolutely. Even though we've recently been repurposed."

"*We've recently been repurposed?*"

"Yup."

"*How* have we been repurposed?"

"Before, we were just straightforward regulators of school and college curricula and exams, you know what I'm saying."

"And?"

"And then somebody told the government that AI was the only game in town, right?"

"Do you think it really is, Aston?"

"I haven't the foggiest. But the government now want us to unleash this AI on education. Trouble is, we know diddly-squat about AI. They nearly abolished us, you know?"

"Really? How awful! Actually, Aston, I've started worrying about this AI, I really have." I then quickly recounted my exasperating experience of trying to register for tax self-assessment with the HMRC. "You see, after I entered my address – my *correct* address – onto the HMRC form, it said that the entered details didn't match their records. But it was *definitely* the right address."

"So why did they reject it?"

"A good question. I couldn't understand it at first, but, then, I twigged: I had simply added the name of my house to the rest of my address."

"So?"

"Well, the address which the HMRC had been using didn't include the name of my house. But, if it had been *a human* checking the form, they would have immediately noticed that the rest of the address was the same. I mean, wouldn't *you* have spotted this?"

"'Course I would, 'course I would."

"Exactly. So my entry *must* have been checked by AI. And it was such a simple thing. Imagine using AI for something more complicated."

"Yup, it's hard to."

"And you know what I've just read?"

"What?"

"That AI is going to take over the world. God help us. Particularly those poor teachers."

"How do you mean?" I thought I could detect suspicion in Aston's voice.

"Well, Crystal told me that the government is trying to replace teachers with AI."

"Shhh! We are not supposed to talk about it – it's *top secret!*"

"But there was nobody else around. We were in the kitchenette."

"Did she check it for bugs?"

"No, there was no need, Aston: it was very clean; I didn't see any creepy-crawlies there."

"No, no, no: I mean wiretaps, hidden microphones,

electronic eavesdroppers, bugging devices, things like that." With that, he sprang up from his chair, dashed towards the door, opened it and poked his head through it, checking for any hostile agents lurking outside. Having reassured himself that there were no moles in the vicinity, he then proceeded to examine the room with a forensic precision. The survey completed to his satisfaction, he returned to his chair, devoured the last chocolate chip biscuit and said: "This is why we have no 'education' in the name of our organisation, right?"

"Actually, I was wondering about this, Aston. But I'm not sure I'm quite with you: why *exactly?*"

"Basically, because our previous Foremost Authoritarian didn't want to alarm teachers, right? So he insisted that we omit 'education' from our name to throw them off the scent."

"Weasel!"

"Wrong animal, Shodra, huh, huh, huh!"

"What do you mean?"

"Fox. His name was Wily Fox, huh, huh, huh!"

"Very apt."

"He also thought it would be best if we kept our name as vague as possible. As a matter of principle."

"I'm... I'm not with you."

"Basically, we are a quango; I've told you, right?"

"You did, but I still can't see why it's best for our name to be vague."

"But I've already told you that they tried to abolish us, right?"

"Yes, but you said that this was because you... because *we* know diddly-squat about AI."

"That also, but being a quango is very precarious by definition, right?"

"But why?"

"Haven't you heard of the 'bonfire of the quangos'?"

"Can't say I have, Aston, no."

"Basically, politicians have been trying to chuck us into this bonfire for yonks."

"But why?"

"Basically, they seem rattled that they are not running the entire show, right? They call us 'quangocracy'."

"So?"

"So they keep saying that they want to claw power back from us. Because we are unelected, right? You know what *The Daily Mail* has been saying?"

"I don't read *The Daily Mail*, Aston."

"*Bonfire of Quangos Long Overdue; May the Wind of Change Sweep Away Quangocracy; Self-serving Bureaucrats Reveal their True Colours; Snouts in Troughs* – stuff like that."

"Oh dear."

"So the government has culled some quangos and renamed others: in our name, they have changed 'regulation' to 'radicalisation', for example."

"Is that good?"

"It should keep us going for a while, you know what I'm saying. But we are still vulnerable."

"Are we really?"

"Absolutely! They've just abolished NHS England, haven't they? The biggest quango of them all, right? And, if they have abolished *them*, what chance have *we* got?"

"Goodness me!"

"And, if they abolish you and you are trying for a job in a completely different sector, you must be able to prove that you have lots of transferable skills."

"How do you prove this?"

"The vaguer the name of your organisation, the harder it is for the new people to pin you down. So, even though you may be attempting to move to a totally unrelated sector, you can insist that your skills will be highly relevant there too. Take our Theo."

"Theo Retic?"

"Nah, Theo Morphic – our Foremost Authoritarian, right?"

"Hmm, not sure what you mean, Aston."

"He's come from sewage."

"It's rather heartening."

"It is indeed, it is indeed."

"Actually, I would say it's inspirational."

"Inspirational? Nah, I wouldn't go that far."

"Why not? For a person to overcome early disadvantage like that…"

"*Disadvantage?* Theo wouldn't know disadvantage if it hit him on the head: private education all the way through, you know what I'm saying."

"But… but you said he'd come from… sewage."

Aston clutched his impressive stomach and gave a deep laugh. "Nah, he's come from the quango overseeing sewage."

"You mean they sacked him?"

"Nah, why would have they done such a thing?"

"Well, look at all this dreadful pollution swirling around our waterways."

"Nah, they don't sack them."

"Whom?"

"The big cheeses."

"They don't?"

"Nah; they just move them, right?"

"You mean demote them?"

"*Demote* them? Nah, they just give them a big fat bonus and make them a boss of a different quango."

"*A boss?* Even if they have a bad record in their job?"

"At that level, their record makes no difference whatsoever, right?"

I must say that I was lost for words, which enabled Aston to continue: "It's called recycling."

"Well, I'm all for recycling, Aston – we have four different bins – but, surely, everyone is supposed to do a good job. Particularly at such a senior level. And, if they fail, there should be consequences."

After Aston finished laughing, he gave me a look full of pity and said: "Consequences are for little people, Shorda. And if you say that you have a pile of transferable skills, sky's the limit. For the bosses, I mean. So sewage can come to education, and education can move to agriculture, for example. But they also look at qualifications. That's why I've got myself an STD. I will shortly try for Enthuser, you know what I'm saying."

"Yes, yes, you definitely should, Aston. A person with your… your capacity to… to enthuse richly deserves to get promoted. Talking about qualifications, I was going to ask you…"

"About what?"

"You know, in this email by Nota…"

"What about it?"

"You know, the letters after her name – are they qualifications?"

"Yup. I've also got them – *all three* of them – you know what I'm saying."

"But… but I don't recognise the acronyms. What do they stand for? This BURP, for example?"

"Business for an Unparalleled Range of Purposes. It's a great introduction to business. For an unparalleled range of purposes, right?"

"Yes, yes, an unparalleled range is always best, Aston."

"Between me and you, it's really just about profit. But, if they said this, fewer people might want this qualification, so they had to jazz it up."

"Yes, yes, I can see that. And what about this DUNG?"

"Diploma in Unravelling the Nature of Governance."

"Does the nature of governance take a lot of unravelling?"

"You'd be surprised, Shorda, you'd be surprised. This diploma should be mandatory for all big cheeses, right?"

"Are you saying it isn't?"

"What do reckon, Zarda? Just look at our institutions. In both public and private sector. All the corruption, cronyism, pandering to vested interests, knighthoods for chums."

"Hmm, that's exactly what Matthew Syed said. In *The Sunday Times*. But wouldn't it be lovely if we could trust our public institutions and politicians?"

"Pigs might fly. Look at all the scandals they either caused or failed to prevent: Windrush, contaminated blood, Hillsborough, parliamentary expenses, honours for cash, Greensill, Partygate, Post Office Horizon IT, Covid procurement – you name it."

"Yes, yes; it's awful."

"And all the cover-ups, you know what I'm saying. Nobody wants to admit that they got things wrong. Certainly not if they risk getting sacked. Or abolished."

"Hmm, maybe they have a mortgage to pay. But, even so, it shouldn't be happening."

"But that's how it is, right? So, whether we like it or not, this is also what *we* have to do. If we don't want to get chucked into this bonfire of the quangos, you know what I'm saying."

"Perish the thought! So what do we have to do *exactly?*"

"Manage and protect our reputation. At all costs. They may call it institutional defensiveness, but it's essential for our survival."

I have to admit that facing a possibility of burning in this fire was rather unnerving, so, rather than dwelling on such an awful prospect, I moved on to the third of Nota's qualifications: "I see, Aston; if you say it's essential, then it must be essential. But what about this DUMB – what does it stand for?"

"Degree in Understanding Motivation in Business. I was their top scholar, you know what I'm saying. I got a first. Nota only got a lower second." A self-satisfying smile playing on his lips, my mentor performed a big stretch accompanied by the tender patting of his belly. In response, his chair creaked threateningly but, thankfully, didn't give way.

"Wow, how impressive, Aston. Could you possibly

give me some idea of motivation in business... in very general terms... I don't expect you to—"

"Greed."

"Greed? And they managed to fashion *a degree* out of it?"

"There's a lot to greed, you know what I'm saying, Sarda – *a lot*."

"Hmm, you are probably right, Aston. Particularly if you're in banking. You know what they say?"

"What do they say?"

"Give a man impunity, and he might rob a bank – give a bank impunity, and it will rob the world."

Aston nodded. "You can say that again."

"Or if you're in politics. All those overnight allowances, tax dodges, duck islands – you mentioned this parliamentary-expenses scandal, didn't you, Aston? I've also heard about it."

"I did indeed, I did indeed. But tax dodges are everywhere, right?"

"Hmm, but maybe they are not *all* tax dodges, Aston. Maybe they were trying to register with the HMRC but, like me, kept being thwarted."

"Maybe, maybe. And she hasn't got an STD, right?"

I was momentarily confused. "Who?"

"Nota." Aston was, clearly, still pondering her credentials and finding them inferior to his.

"So how come she got promoted over you?"

Aston smirked. "Basically, her and Theo... you know what I'm saying."

"Yes, yes, Crystal did mention something along those lines. Things like that shouldn't really..."

At that moment, there was a knock on the door.

"That will be the lunch," said Aston, performing the stretch-pat routine again. "Come on in."

"Good afternoon. I've got your lunch," said the lunch lady, wheeling in a trolley full of trays sitting alongside a few vessels.

"Thank you, Victoria," said Aston, eyeing the trolley hungrily and swallowing hard.

There were four trays with sandwiches, one tray with panini, one with pizza slices, one with pigs in blankets, one with scotch eggs and one with pasties. There was also a fruit platter and a plate of cupcakes. In addition, we got two large bags of crisps and two thermoses – one with coffee and one with tea – and two jugs – one with cream and the other with milk.

"Semi-skimmed," explained Victoria, "but I can also get you skimmed, full-fat, soya or almond."

"Thank you, Victoria, cream will do me. Zadra?"

"Nothing else, nothing else, thank you."

Victoria nodded, smiled and left.

"Gosh, that's a banquet – who's joining us, Aston?"

"Nobody's joining us."

"But we'll never be able to eat *all* of that, surely."

"But we'll have a jolly good try, huh, huh, huh! That's what we normally get; courtesy of BT."

"British Telecom? I didn't realise they were *that* generous."

"No, no, no: British taxpayers. British taxpayers have deep pockets – even in these straitened times, huh, huh, huh! Basically, you have to cater for all the tastes and preferences. In this day and age, some people are quite…

quite fragile. I mean, I'll eat anything, but not everyone is that robust. And I didn't know about you. Besides, we often get people popping in just to get some free grub. Some even bring a doggy bag."

"Well, at least the leftovers won't go to waste, Aston."

My mentor nodded. "Basically, this is our standard selection. Look, this is meat on white, this is meat on brown, this is tuna on white, this is tuna on brown, this is vegetarian, this is vegan and this is gluten-free. Our Catering Department is first class."

"We have a Catering Department?"

"We do indeed, we do indeed. Frank Furter does a grand job, you know what I'm saying."

"Who is Frank Furter?"

"Head of our Catering Department. But his staff are also excellent."

"How many people work for him?"

"Six: Victoria Sponge – she has brought our lunch – Sugar Loaf, Al Fresco, Ala Carte, Barbie Turate and Ana Bolic. They are a great bunch. Tuck in."

With that, Aston attacked several trays simultaneously, piling his plate high with pigs in blankets, sandwiches, pizza slices and pasties. When he tried to put a panino on the very top, it fell off, disintegrating all over the table.

"Sorry, Zarda, I need another plate. Anyways, time is pressing on, so we might as well have a working lunch. We often have working lunches, you know what I'm saying."

"How often?"

"As often as we can. When you schedule your meetings to coincide with lunchtime, you get a free lunch, right?"

"What a… what a clever strategy."

"It ish, it ish, mmm, thish ish delicioush." Although Aston was determinedly munching on a large slice of pizza, he gave every impression of being well versed in speaking with his mouth full. There was one male who could multitask, I thought. Good on him. Nevertheless, I decided that it would be advisable to let him enjoy his food uninterrupted, so, having eaten my sandwich – tuna on brown – followed by five grapes and four strawberries, I kept quiet while observing Aston carry out a comprehensive demolition job on Victoria's trays. When I thought that it would be beyond any human's capacity to consume any more, I decided to resume the working bit of our working lunch. I was, however, slightly premature.

"Actually, Aston, I was going to ask—"

"Yesh? Theshe pashties are moorish. Oops, shorry, Schubra." A small segment of a pasty flew across the table and landed right on my nose. Aston passed me a napkin with an apologetic smile, finished the pasty, wiped a blob of mayonnaise off the end of his moustache, smacked his lips, burped contentedly and performed yet another stretch-pat routine. I brushed the pasty spit from my nose.

"Crystal said that, in addition to harvesting all the stuff for AI, we also have to write tons of reports. She did actually explain why, but I would appreciate your take on it. I mean, it seems to me that…"

At this point, the door opened and in strode a besuited gentleman wearing an executive look on his face.

"Hiya, guys! Oh, lunch – what a nice surprise."

I have to say that I couldn't detect much surprise in the man's voice, but one mustn't jump to conclusions. I've already said this much, haven't I?

"Hello, Inco, come on it, come on in."

But Aston was slightly too late with his invite because the visitor was already reaching for a pig in a blanket: Aston had left some of those.

"Inco, meet Shorda. Zadra has just joined us; she is Polish. I'm delivering my induction training to her. Zhudra, this is Inco. Inco Herent. Our Supreme Enthuser."

"Pleased to meet you, Mr Herent."

Inco nodded and looked me up and down in what some might have interpreted as a rather politically incorrect manner. Thankfully, I wasn't like Millie; boys will be boys. Unless they are girls.

Aston continued: "We are having a working lunch, Inco."

Having probably concluded that I wasn't much to look at – and who could blame him? – Inco quickly turned towards Aston and nodded again.

"Shorda was just asking me about our reports, Inco, and here you are! I'm sure you will be able to elucidate infinitely better than me – *infinitely* better!"

Inco couldn't answer immediately because his mouth was full of a scotch egg, so another nod was entirely appropriate. This gave me the chance to reflect on Aston's obsequiousness: he seemed to be rather full of himself, so I didn't have him down as a bootlicker. Then again, he said he was going to go for Enthuser, and, when harbouring such lofty ambitions, one probably couldn't overdo on deference.

Two more scotch eggs and three sandwiches later, Inco reached for a napkin and looked at me again – albeit no longer probingly. "So what particulars necessitate particular elucidation, Sho... Zhu... thingy?"

"Why do we have to write all these reports?"

"So, yes, it is judgmatical to circumstantiate the process."

"*Circumstantiate?*"

"Basically, Inco means to document the process, Shadra. It's important to be able to prove that we have followed it."

Inco nodded: "Literatim."

"*Literatim?*"

"Basically, Inco means 'to the letter.'"

Inco nodded again.

"But why, Inco?"

"So, yes, there is nothing more puissant than process," elucidated Inco.

"*Puissant?*"

"Basically, Inco means important."

"Thank you, Aston. But I thought it was outcome?"

"Nah, the process is an end in itself, right?"

At this juncture, Inco got up and announced: "Must away. I'm cognizant Aston will perdure with his epexegesis. Adios, guys."

And with this, somewhat baffling, announcement, he swept the remaining contents of three of Victoria's trays into his doggy bag, which he had deftly procured from somewhere about his person, and was gone. I must admit to a certain amount of relief that I would no longer require an interpreter and saw Aston in a new light: at least you could understand what the man was saying.

"But why isn't an outcome important, Aston?"

"Basically, with an outcome, things can go wrong. Even badly wrong – you can never be quite sure, right?

Particularly if you don't know what you are doing. You may be planning to achieve one thing and end up with a completely different one. And far worse at that, right?"

"You mean like with Brexit?"

"Absolutely, absolutely! But you can always hide behind processes and procedures."

"Actually, this is *exactly* what Crystal said."

A broad self-satisfied smile lit up Aston's face. "And she was *absolutely* right, you know what I'm saying. You can see just how well I mentored her. If things go badly wrong, all you need to do is say that you have followed all the processes and procedures to the letter, so whatever has gone wrong couldn't *possibly* be your fault."

"Yes, yes, Crystal did say the same thing."

"Basically, it's all about creating a paper trail so that you can use it in your defence. In case you are sued. Or threatened with abolition. I've told you about institutional defensiveness, right?"

"Yes, yes, Aston, you have."

"Basically, the same goes for individuals."

"Actually, Aston, I did read something along those lines in *The Sunday Times*."

"Oh yes, what did they write?"

"That colorectal doctors spend more time covering arses than treating them."

Aston nodded. "Yup; we all gotta do it. But, in your reports, you should also be as ambiguous as possible. Just in case, right?"

"Hmm, yes, Crystal said this too. But I must say I feel rather sorry for the readers, Aston. They will be baffled."

"Who cares? Our readers aren't our main concern."

"So what is our main concern?"

My mentor appeared annoyed. "I've told you: to keep our jobs! You will definitely need more training. The CID will take care of you."

"*I beg your pardon?*"

"They will sort you out."

"Oh please, no – not the CID: *I don't know anything!*"

"That's *exactly* your problem, Shorba."

"So… so why do you… do you want to involve the Criminal Investigation…?"

"No, no, no: it's our *Corporate Inductions Department*, right?"

"Oh, I s-e-e-e-e, thank goodness!"

6

Huddles, Aliens and Bombs

"ICH, ICH!" exclaimed Aston as soon as he entered the office the following morning. Keen to make a good impression, I was already there, getting properly acquainted with my desk, but I must say that my mentor's revelation jolted me bolt upright.

"How awful, Aston; I'm so sorry."

"No need to be, no need to be."

"How... how long have you had it?"

"Have *what?*"

"This... this intracerebral haemorrhage."

"*What haemorrhage?*"

"Well, you've just said ICH, haven't you?"

"No, no, no, I meant our Intimate Cluster Huddle, right? That's what we start each working day with. To foster better teamwork and engender communal spirit in our cluster. So that we are more productive and write more reports than any other cluster, you know what I'm saying."

Relieved, I wondered if this was Aston's way of

accumulating brownie points towards his promotion to Enthuser.

During our exchange, a few more colleagues entered the office, but Dali, who was also already sitting behind her desk, intervened: "But, Aston, Stu, like, ain't 'ere yet." She then immediately corrected herself: "Stu ain't 'ere yet."

I was mightily impressed by how quickly she had taken my advice about fillers on board. The young lady will go far, no question. But I was surprised that a guy from procurement should participate in our ICH.

"You mean Stu Peed, Dali? I thought he worked in procurement."

The girl shook her head. "No, no, *our* Stu – Stu Pendous."

"Oh, I see."

"There he is, there he is," said Aston, pointing at a middle-aged gentleman with a mop of wavy hair sauntering towards the desk next to Millie's.

"Morning, morning, morning, all."

"Stu, meet Zobra; she joined us yesterday. Sorba, this is Stu."

"Morning, Stu; how are you?"

"Fit as a butcher's dog and twice as hairy, ho, ho, ho!" Stu had a deep throaty laughter, and, when he chortled, his eyes sparkled.

"Our ICH, our ICH!" insisted Aston.

There were now quite a few of us, including Viv, Theo, Ira and Ant, to whom I was introduced the previous afternoon, after we had all returned from our respective meetings. Following Aston's directive, we all quickly formed a tight circle, each of us putting our arm around the waist of each of our two neighbours. Or, in some cases, attempted to but failed: I had the honour of bordering Aston, but to reach all the way around *his* waist proved to be a sheer impossibility. I thus grabbed at the back of his jacket and hoped for the best; thankfully, there were no repercussions. Having fostered better teamwork and engendered communal spirit, we released our respective grips.

I then tried to make small talk with Stu by way of breaking the ice – not that I detected any ice around him. "Aston said you were from Ireland – which part?"

"All of me: from top to toe, ho, ho, ho!"

This Stu was going to be fun to be around, I quickly decided.

"I find the Irish delightful, Stu: my husband is from Dublin. He is very laid back – doesn't do stress at all."

"Neither do I – unless my missus goes completely bonkers in the sales. Until a man is married, he is incomplete. Then, he's finished – ho, ho, ho!"

"Just don't tell my husband, ha, ha, ha!"

"To be sure, Sho… Zo… Cobra."

Now, when your first name is Szczodra, where *exactly* do you draw the line? Obviously, you take it as a given that the natives will mispronounce it, but was I going to be able to get used to Cobra? Suddenly, I had a brainwave. I do have brainwaves sometimes. Not often – but it does happen.

"Why don't you call me Ali?"

Aston gave me a look expressing a mixture of surprise and annoyance and demanded: "Ali? Your name is *Ali?* So why did you subject us to all these verbal gymnastics? I nearly twisted my tongue, you know what I'm saying."

"No, no, Ali isn't my *real* name, but it's nice and easy, isn't it?"

"It is, but why do you suddenly want us to call you Ali?"

"I need to tell you a little anecdote…"

"We have no time for your little anecdotes, right?" barked my mentor.

"But my anecdote is very relevant – it explains about Ali."

"Make it quick, you know what I'm saying."

My colleagues' faces assumed a mask of eager anticipation, and I commenced my tale. "Well, decades ago, when I landed at Heathrow, they had these two signs there. One sign said *British Nationals*, and the other said *Aliens*. So I had to queue up with all these other aliens to have my passport and visa checked, and this memorable sign has stayed with me for all those years."

"Your point being?" demanded Aston impatiently.

"Well, you take the word *alien*, you discard the last two letters, and you end up with *ali*. So you can easily convert it into Ali, and – voilà – you have an easy name."

"But, in this day and age, we don't call aliens aliens in this country," protested Millie. "Actually, you cannot even say 'aliens,'" she quickly corrected herself.

"But this was *ages* ago, Millie."

"Even so. If I was you—"

"Were."

"Where what?"

"No, no, not where – *were*. If I *were* you, Millie."

"What would you do?"

"No, no, *I* wouldn't do anything, but—"

"So let me finish please. As I was saying, if I was you, I wouldn't go round calling aliens aliens. I mean using this word."

I momentarily wondered if Millie was losing her grip on things, what with her repeatedly using a proscribed word herself.

"But it's just an innocent little anecdote explaining about Ali."

"Mug – definitely a mug," opined Aston.

"Oh, Aston, I may not be the *sharpest* tool in the box, but I haven't yet been openly called a mug by anybody. At least not—"

"No, no, no – it's a *Most Unsafe Game*: MUG. Basically, it starts as an innocent little anecdote and ends up in court, you know what I'm saying. We live in a litigious culture."

"Oh dear, does it really end up in court, Aston?"

"It does indeed, it does indeed."

"How come?"

"Basically, you start calling aliens aliens, and they get hold of one of these no-win-no-fee outfits, and, before you know it, you are being done for a major injury to feelings and a profound psychological trauma, you know what I'm saying. And sued for big bucks. Do you think we want to get dragged through the courts? And jeopardise our government grant?"

"Perish the thought, Aston. Look, why don't you just forget my little anecdote and call me Ali simply because my real name is unpronounceable. Perhaps Ali could be my assumed name…"

"Numb the plum!" exclaimed Mala, nodding her head.

I must admit that I failed to see how her suggestion vis-à-vis the unfortunate plum fitted into our confabulation. "Why would you want to numb this plum, Mala?"

At this very point, Crystal performed an energetic 180-degree turn in her chair. I looked at her back and could see her shoulders convulsing spasmodically.

"Uh? Rewind," demanded Mala.

"She, ha, ha, ha, she means... she means *nom de plume*," roared Crystal.

"That's *exactly* what I said."

"Of course, of course, Mala. Yes, we could pretend that Ali is my *nom de plume:* I do write books."

"I'm liking it," announced my frizzy-haired colleague after appearing to ponder the proposition for a brief moment.

"So are you all OK with calling me Ali? After all, Theo has changed his name, so I can change mine."

"Yep; let's go for Ali," agreed Crystal.

"Cool beans," concurred Dew.

"Defo," echoed Dali.

"Aye, aye, nae bother," said Jock.

Stu was also in agreement: "To be sure, to be sure."

"Yup, we'll give it a go, Shod... Ali," declared Aston.

"As long as you don't mention the 'A' word," cautioned me Millie.

Other colleagues having also expressed their approval by the execution of vigorous nods, I would henceforth be known as Ali. Blast, I should have thought of this right at the start. But better late than never.

Before we got back to our desks, Stu smiled at me and asked: "Do you like jokes, Ali?"

"Of course – doesn't everyone? But I can never remember them for long."

"I'm your man, then; I know lots of jokes. Your woman says to her friend, 'I'm looking for a good plastic surgeon,' to which the friend replies, 'Wouldn't you prefer a real one?' Your man phones the local council. 'May I have a skip in front of my house?' The council official responds, 'You may turn cartwheels for all I care.' This vicar unveils a new slogan in his church, 'I Upped My Pledge – Up Yours.' A sergeant major is telling off a young soldier, 'Jones, I didn't see you at camouflage training this morning,' to which the soldier replies, 'Thank you, sir.' They had these two advertisements in the paper: 'We do not tear your clothing with machinery. We do it carefully by hand' and 'Used Cars: Why go elsewhere to be cheated? Come here first.'"

There was no doubt that I was going to get on with Stu I concluded en route to my desk. And it occurred to me that he may have called me Cobra for a joke. Anyway, it was for the best. Other colleagues also took up their positions for the day, but, before we could demonstrate the positive impact of Aston's intimate cluster huddle on our productivity, the air was pierced by a female voice.

Everybody looked around: it was Mala, who was peering at her computer screen and shaking her head. "I so don't believe this!"

Having been given my own password, I quickly logged in. Crystal leant towards me, pointed to the communication near the bottom of my screen and said, "Read this."

The email was entitled: *BASE-LESS AND SCURRILUS RUMORS – CRITICAL URGENT*. It read:

Colleagues,

It has COME, to our attention that some BASE-LESS, rumors' about FART, have started CIRCULATING among teachers'. Those RUMORS', seem to have now been picked up by, the PRESS. Please click on the link at the BOTTOM, of this email for an article, in todays issue of The Educationalist. We CANNOT allow to, have the name of, our organisation BE-SMIRCHED and are urgently INVESTIGATING, who is the source of this MIS-INFORMATION. There will be an EXTRA ORDINARY MEETING, at the Grand Central Metropolitan at noon, today. Attendance is COMPULSATORY, for all Directorates' and FRONT line staff. Agency STAFF, will be DEPLOYED to man the phones. Lunch, will be PROVIDED.

Regards.
Inco Municado.
Director of Communications.
Communications Directorate.
FART.

"Goodness me, this... this Inco Municado is actually in charge of our *communications*, Crystal?"

"Yep, ha, ha, ha!" roared my fellow alien.

"Had he gone to the same school as Trump, by any chance?"

Crystal continued laughing. "His adjutants are just as bad."

"Who are they?"

"Arti Culator, Cari Cature and Ana Bridged. But Arti is watching."

"Whom?"

"Inco. He is waiting for Inco to slip up so that he can take over; he is very ambitious."

Not unlike Aston, I reflected before suggesting: "Now is Arti's chance then."

"In what way?"

"Well, this email… Surely, it's a huge slip-up by Inco?"

"Nope. They all write like this, ha, ha, ha! Wait till you see what has been penned by our Phillis Tine and Ignor Amus – and how they will correct your writing, ha, ha, ha!"

"Who are they?"

"Our editors."

"We have editors?"

"We have an entire Editorial Department, ha, ha, ha!"

"Isn't that good? All writing benefits from being edited. I should know: I write books."

"The only people who benefit are Molly Coddle and Val Erian, ha, ha, ha!"

"The ones from our Wellness Department?"

"Them ones, them ones, as our Dali might say."

"Actually, I'm going to teach Dali and Dew a little bit of grammar. They seemed quite receptive. It would be such a shame to squander latent talent."

"Perhaps you could also include Phillis, Ignor & Co., but you would have to make it a big bit, ha, ha, ha!"

"Well, I would need to see their writing and editing first."

"Be careful what you wish for, Ali! And book yourself an appointment with Molly and Val."

"Why?"

"After you've seen how our editors have mutilated your writing, you are likely to have to go into therapy, ha, ha, ha!"

It took me a while to digest this unsettling revelation. When I recovered, I asked Crystal: "Where is this Grand Central Metropolitan?"

"Just round the corner. That's where we have many of our meetings. Unless it's fully booked. But all the hotels we use are five-star anyway, so it's much of a muchness."

I clicked on the link in Inco's email and started reading the article.

FART under a Cloud of Suspicion

After repeatedly thwarting all attempts at independent scrutiny of its murky activities, the recently rebranded Foremost Authority for the Radicalisation of Transformation (FART) seems to be engaging in a large-scale operation aiming to undermine the teaching profession throughout Britain. The exact nature of the operation hasn't yet been ascertained, but our sources have informed us that its goal is to implement revolutionary changes to the profession underpinned by a wide-spread use of AI. The largest teaching union, SMUT, has requested a meeting with FART's Foremost Authoritarian to seek an urgent clarification of the proposed reform, which, it is rumoured, might be enforced as early as next year. SMUT's General Secretary, Mr Rod Iron, told our reporter, "Although we are as yet unclear as to the exact nature of the radicalisation of transformation currently being undertaken by FART, my members are concerned that the profession will be further destabilised by yet another upheaval." The Educationalist will be monitoring the situation closely and will be bringing you the news of the developments as they unfold.

"What does SMUT stand for exactly, Crystal?"
"Sagacious and Meritorious Union of Teachers."

***

As noon approached, Aston said: "Let's go: we don't want to be late."

"We'd better 'ave a man Ant," chirruped Dali.

I must admit that I was rather puzzled. Ant was among the colleagues to whom I had been introduced the previous afternoon.

"Why, Dali? We *do* have a man Ant."

"No, no: not a man *Ant*, a *man* Ant."

"What's the difference?"

"A *man* Ant, a *man* Ant!"

"All right, all right; just give us a little clue."

"'Cos Theo's gone missin', and we 'ave to go see Inco in a sec, lik… uhm."

Realising that Dali's elucidation had failed to enlighten me, Crystal galloped to the rescue, albeit with a chuckle:

"She means 'manhunt', Ali. Because Theo has disappeared, and we all have to go now."

Dali nodded. "He's armless, li… but likes to go missin', innit?"

Now, if someone had heard Dali for the first time, they would undoubtedly have been overcome with sympathy for this armless Theo, but I knew better now. I faced a dilemma, however: how do I explain to the girl the effect of her pronunciation without upsetting her? One's way of speaking is such a personal thing – I should know – but it would be an awful shame if hers should hold her back. I reflected on Professor Higgins with his hurricanes which hardly ever happened and decided that I needed a subtler approach. But it wasn't going to be easy. On the other hand, Dali obviously had potential: she was in the office before Aston, and now she has taken the manhunt initiative without being prompted. Why do they let them leave school like that? But maybe she didn't go to school. I understand they didn't use to monitor home-schoolers – *if* Dali received any home-schooling, that is. Much as I would have liked to ponder the wider picture for a while longer, I couldn't ignore my interlocutors.

"Yes, yes, do go on your manhunt, Dali."

"Sick!" With this, the girl sprang up from her chair and made for the door.

"We'd better go, Ali; I'm sure Theo will materialise at some stage," said Crystal. The entire floor emptied, and we all trooped downstairs: the lift had broken down again. It took us only a few minutes to reach the plush hotel. Once inside, I could see that everybody knew exactly where they were going. Actually, it wasn't all that difficult – you would simply follow your nose. In the large lobby on the first floor, tables were groaning under the weight of various bowls, trays, plates, platters, baskets, jugs and thermoses, a pleasant smell of cooked food wafting through the air.

"Mmm, nice smell," murmured Aston, helping himself to an ultra-generous portion of sizzling lasagne topped with a humongous helping of steaming haggis.

"There's usually hot and cold, Ali," helpfully explained Mala. "Go ahead, ladies: don't be pussy animals."

"*I beg your pardon?*"

"She means *pusillanimous*." It was clear that my aptly named colleague's malaprops held no mystery for Crystal. Mindful of our respective waistlines, she, Stu, Millie and I made for the salads.

"I have two gastronomic jokes for you,' said Stu. "Your man goes into an ice-cream parlour demanding a refund: 'I keep buying Death by Chocolate, but it hasn't worked so far.' The ice-cream seller replies, 'You probably need a higher dose. Three scoops this time?' A chef asks a trainee, 'How do you sex a crab?' The trainee replies, 'I don't know; I've only ever seen them dressed.'"

When we stopped chuckling, I asked, "Apropos jokes, this *Bomb Threat Checklist* – is it a joke? We are not supposed to take it seriously, surely?"

"We are, we are, to be sure." With his usual chortle, Ant quickly seized this opportunity to tell us a bomb joke. "Ben and Joe are walking across a field, find three unexploded bombs and decide to take them to the police station. Off they go with the bombs tucked under their arms – as you do – but, suddenly, Ben stops and asks, 'What are we going to do if we drop one, and it explodes?' Joe replies, 'Don't worry, we'll tell them we've found only two.'"

But you know what, I've just realised that I haven't told you about my starter pack yet. And, without this crucial piece of intelligence, the aforementioned *Bomb Threat Checklist* wouldn't have made much sense to you. I imagine you were baffled – go on, admit it. So here goes. I was supposed to fill the interval before the receipt of Inco's missive and our EXTRA ORDINARY MEETING with a perusal of my starter pack, which had been handed to me by Aston with considerable solemnity. The pack comprised a thick wodge of documents.

"Here is your starter pack, Ali; general workplace instructions, rules, regulations, forms, stuff like that. You've got until noon to get to grips with that lot."

The wodge contained many colourful booklets, one of which aroused my particular interest: *Driving at Work – Managing Work-Related Road Safety*. Given that Aston had his nose buried in his own pile of papers, I directed my initial enquiry at Mala.

"How do you distinguish work-related road safety from non-work-related road safety?"

"Uh?"

"This booklet is on work-related road safety."

"Hmm… you… you just concentrate on work-related road safety and don't worry about any other safety – just forget all about it. Read the booklet – it's all in there."

"But would that be relevant to me, do you think?"

"'Course it would be relevent to you; it's relevent to everybody."

"But I don't drive, Mala."

"Why?"

"Because I *cannot* drive: I've never learnt."

"How do you mean *you've never learnt?*"

"How can you learn to drive when your brake is next to your accelerator? Lethal! And all those confusing gears. Besides, the natives drive on the wrong side of the road, though – admittedly – to them… I mean to *you* it's right. But it's actually left – quite disorientating. I had loads of lessons, but they didn't seem to work. I nearly mowed a pedestrian down and drove into a huge stone wall. My driving instructor had to have a big shot of valerian after that – he said he kept it for exceptional occasions."

"Poor instructor." Did I detect more amusement than sympathy in Crystal's voice?

"And when you refuse to drive faster than 35mph along an A road, the other drivers are so rude it's unbelievable. They sit on your tail and hoot the horn non-stop. And when they overtake you, they make this rude gesture. You know, with two fingers. Some even shout abuse. Awful, absolutely awful. Very un-British, if you ask me."

"So did you fail your driving test?" enquired Mala.

"I never got as far as the test. After a year – maybe a bit longer – I decided that driving just wasn't for me. I got the impression that my instructor agreed: he couldn't stop smiling when I told him. Then again, he was a smiley person anyway, so I might have got the wrong impression."

"I'm sure he was devastated, ha, ha, ha!"

"Thank you, Crystal. Actually, I described my travails in one of my funny books. It's called *Lakeland Larks, Laughter and Lunacies of an Unmotorised Lake District Walker*. It has been published by The Book Guild."

"I'm going to get it, Ali; where do they sell it?" asked Crystal.

"You can get it from any bookshop. And online: it's on Amazon and many other websites. How about you, Mala?"

"Nah, I don't read books."

"But... but this booklet on driving – do you think I should still read it?"

"Yea: they say we have to be like Fay with it."

"Who's Fay?"

"The one we have to be like."

"Am I going to meet her soon, Mala?"

"She means *au fait*: we are supposed to be *au fait* with the stuff in this booklet, ha, ha, ha!" On this occasion, Crystal didn't attempt to suppress her chuckle.

The above expectation notwithstanding, I decided to leave *Driving at Work – Managing Work-Related Road Safety* for last and to tackle other aspects of health and safety head on. The health-and-safety booklets were accompanied by a FART publication entitled *Guidelines for the Clarification and Amplification of Health and Safety Rules, Regulations and Principals*. While clumsily written, the Guidelines were very comprehensive, laying out FART's clarification and amplification in a series of chapters. The chapter which grabbed my attention particularly violently was that on *Bomb Threats:* as Aston might say, you cannot be too careful in this day and age. There was also the *Bomb Threat Checklist* there. Judging by the questions it posed, the *Bomb Threat Checklist* was designed for the person receiving a phone notification of a bomb threat. Did the checklist apply also to cluster bombs? I giggled to myself. Now, if you should ever find yourself answering a call advising you about a bomb planted in your office, I imagine you would find the questions listed in this checklist helpful. And, of course, any terrorist would undoubtedly be keen to answer them. They went like this:

1. Where is the bomb located?
2. When is it going to explode?
3. What does it look like?
4. What kind of bomb is it?
5. What will cause it to explode?
6. Did you place the bomb?
7. Why did you place the bomb?
8. When did you place the bomb?
9. How did you place the bomb?
10. Who did you place the bomb with?
11. Where are you calling from?
12. What is your name?
13. What is your postal address?
14. What is your email address?
15. What is your landline telephone number?
16. What is your mobile telephone number?

For a brief moment, I wondered why they hadn't included a question about the caller's bank details and their mother's maiden name, but my attention was drawn to the reverse of the form, which was supposed to be completed once the caller had hung up and the Facilities' Manager had been informed. I made a mental note to find out, as a matter of the utmost urgency, who our Facilities' Manager was. This side of the form listed a range of categories, and you were supposed to circle that option in each category which best matched your caller. This read as follows:

1. **Caller**: male, female, third sex, adult, juvenile, familiar. (This left me wondering what to circle if the caller should happen to be unfamiliar. And how would you establish that the caller was of a third sex? You would definitely need Millie's assistance with this one.)
2. **Voice**: local, soft, rough, hoarse, educated, high pitch, deep, nasal, lisp, disguised. (Again, why did they not countenance the possibility that the voice might *not* be local?)
3. **Speech**: fast, slow, distinct, taped, slurred, stutter. (If the speech was taped, who exactly was supposed to answer your questions? You can't have a conversation with a tape.)
4. **Language**: obscene, coarse, normal, educated. (Were they implying that educated language wasn't exactly normal? If not, how could you tell normal language?)
5. **Accent**: local, regional, foreign. (This also got me a bit frazzled: my Polish ear isn't particularly good at guessing where people come from in this wonderful country. Perhaps terrorists should be advised not to call aliens such as me.)
6. **Manner**: calm, angry, rational, irrational, coherent, incoherent/drunk, deliberate, hysterical, aggravated, humorous. (What was rational to one person might be quite irrational to another, I thought. Take Brexit, for example. And would it be rational or irrational for a person to tell you that you were about to be blasted to smithereens by a bomb?)

7. **Background Noises**: road traffic, house noises, animal noises, office, factory, PA system, crockery, party atmosphere, quiet, other, voices, music, static, motor. (I must admit that I didn't have a clue as to what static background noises were. But at least you could circle 'other'.)

The above misgivings notwithstanding, I couldn't help feeling reassured that FART was preparing me so thoroughly for the challenges which lay ahead.

7

Moles, Accents, Unconscious Biases and Predictors of Beaconicity

You now find us back at the Grand Central Metropolitan, where we are devouring the sumptuous lunch laid on for us. Actually, the devouring was being carried out by Aston, our small contingent, stationed by the salads, being rather more restrained. I had been given to understand that we were regulars, so the hotel was well acquainted with our corporate appetite, which, let's face it, seemed rather rapacious. At least judging by the two lunches I have had the good fortune to partake in over the past two days. In fact, I marvelled how it was possible that not everyone was Aston's size and resolved to exercise utmost gastronomical discipline lest I should soon require a whole new wardrobe in a larger size. But the grub was definitely a perk; perhaps it was worth working for FART after all, its transformational synergies and blueprints notwithstanding.

Our little group having subsequently migrated to the neighbouring sweets, Mala pointed at one of the colourful platters and gasped. "Look, look, they've given us coconut cake; we've never had coconut cake before "

"You are triggering me, you are triggering me," exclaimed Millie, raising her hands to her temple in a rather dramatic gesture.

"Why?"

"You can't possibly say this!"

"Uh? Rewind?"

"You can't say… say the 'C' word!"

"*What 'C' word? Cake?*"

"No, no!" Millie's voice now became a virtual whisper. "You know… coconut."

"But why?"

"Because it's…"

At this precise juncture, a wave of excitement rippled through the entire lobby, so our attention was distracted.

"It's Inco, it's Inco. He says to go in."

Obediently, we trooped in. The conference room was of a size befitting a conference room. On the podium stood a table and a chair, and, on the table, there was a jug of water, a glass and a projector connected to a laptop. On the wall behind the podium was a large screen. We grabbed our seats, each cluster clustering together. Aston had chosen a row of chairs roughly in the middle, so that's where we parked ourselves. As is customary on similar occasions, the first row was left empty. When we were all seated, in walked a tall, rake-thin gentleman in a sharp suit.

"That's Inco," whispered Crystal.

Inco took the podium.

"Afternoon, troops. As you will have perceived from my email, we have a crisis on our hands. A *serious* crisis. But, before we start, the front row looks rather empty." The gaze which Inco cast across the entire room alighted on the colleagues in the back row. "Would the troops at the back please reposition to the front; I don't bite."

I had to admire Aston's foresight: we were entirely safe ensconced in the middle.

The resettlement completed, Inco resumed his exposition. "I take it you have all perused the article in today's *Educationalist?*"

Everybody nodded, with Aston nodding perhaps a few times more than was necessitated by the occasion.

"Good. But their allegation is a complete and utter fabrication. As far as the outside world is concerned, anyway. This is our official line, and we are supposed to stick to it until the government is ready to come clean. Is this comprehended?"

Everybody nodded, with Aston again nodding a few times more than was strictly necessary.

"Now, let me put this to you: do you know who the source of this deleterious leak might be?"

We all shifted in our chairs and looked at one another. Aston even looked at the row behind, whose occupants reciprocated with hostile stares of their own and several tut-tuts. A few uncomfortable moments passed, but nobody volunteered an answer. Inco's gaze again swept across the entire room – this time, more deliberately.

"All right then, I can see that nobody is going to own up. But I'm warning you: when the culprit is discovered, the consequences will be most severe – *most* severe. In the meantime, our most pressing concern is to contain the crisis. FART is going to take out full-page denials in all major national newspapers. And, if anybody receives any queries from schools, SMUT or the press about this, they must immediately escalate them to me. Don't get involved in any explanations. Under any circumstances. No comments whatsoever. And you mustn't discuss this with anybody outside our organisation – *anybody*. Is this comprehended?"

We all nodded, with Aston nodding so vigorously I feared he might do himself a nasty brain injury.

"I would also suggest that married colleagues sleep in separate bedrooms. At least until further notice."

A discernible ripple of consternation spread across the entire room, with the audience clearly unable to conceal its bafflement.

"But… but why?" This brave enquiry came from Ant.

"Because people often talk in their sleep. So they can inadvertently blurt out all sorts of stuff. Remember, this is top secret – highly classified."

"But… but what if people don't have a second bedroom?" On this occasion, the courageous questioner was Viv. I had spoken to Ant and Viv only briefly when we were being introduced the previous afternoon, but I must say that I was most impressed. In fact, I was delighted that they were in my cluster: maybe their fearlessness will rub off on me.

"They could always put up a camp bed in the living room," replied Inco without a moment's hesitation. "Remember, every single one of us has a role to play. On my behalf, I have just authorised a thorough de-bugging operation throughout our offices. In fact, it has just started, so I don't want anyone back at their desk yet. For the next couple of hours, you are to remain here. I have ordered afternoon refreshments for everybody. Is this comprehended?"

Guess who was nodding with an utmost vigour.

"That will be all, troops."

I couldn't believe my ears: even *more* refreshments! As soon as Inco left, I asked Crystal: "Why did he say 'on my behalf'?"

"Oh, that's a common mistake. Quite a few folk here say 'on my behalf' when they mean 'on my part'."

"Even Inco?"

"*Particularly* Inco," roared Crystal.

All the clusters, still keeping together, dispersed throughout the conference room and the adjacent lobby, from which the remnants of our lunch were being removed, with the tables being set up for the afternoon refreshments. Most of our cluster migrated to one of the corners of the room, although Aston returned to the lobby. Could it have been that he wanted to get first dibs on the forthcoming refreshments?

I reflected on Inco's de-bugging operation. If it's sufficiently thorough, they should also find any unexploded bombs – surely. So that's one thing fewer to worry about.

"Did they, lik… did they really call you an alien?" enquired Dali.

Thankfully, Millie had just popped out for a comfort break, so Dali's question failed to provoke a violent reaction.

"They did, they did. Not just me: anyone who came from abroad was called an alien."

"And now the boot is on the other foot. Britain has become a third country, so we are third-country nationals."

Crystal seemed to agree with Viv. "Yep, native Britons are effectively aliens in Europe. In the Schengen Area, they now have two lines: one says *EU* and the other *All Passports*, so Brits have a lot of time to ponder all the amazing Brexit benefits as they queue up at passport control. But at least the Europeans are more diplomatic."

Stu chortled. "To be sure, to be sure. And, when you stand shoulder to shoulder with travellers from Bolivia, Burundi and Bangladesh and your passport queue barely moves, you have this marvellous opportunity to strike up all sorts of conversations. You may even find you have a lot in common and become buddies. That's why Brexiteers want us to call this country global Britain, ho, ho, ho!"

Crystal smiled. "But we are fine."

"Who?" asked Dali.

"Ali, Stu and me. Poland, Ireland and Denmark all allow dual citizenship, so we are still EU nationals. Think about it: even though the three of us are first-generation immigrants, we have retained our European rights and freedoms. And native Britons have actually voted to curb their own – you couldn't make it up."

"Proper mingin," reflected Dali.

"That's why getting hold of an EU passport has become the holy grail for Brits – particularly the young ones. To be able to live on the Continent for more than ninety days, to travel freely, to study or to work without restrictions. What's not to like?"

Stu concurred with our Danish friend. "To be sure, to be sure: it's a golden ticket to freedom. Everyone tries to rustle up a grandparent born in what is now an EU country."

"But some countries don't let you go that far back: it has to be a parent," added Viv.

"Actually, some countries don't allow dual citizenship at all," clarified Theo, who definitely wasn't armless. "But many do. Do you know that, between 2016 and 2022, nearly 80,000 Brits acquired a European passport?"

Stu shook his head. "But, Theo, that doesn't include applications for Irish citizenship. In 2022 alone, there were 100,000 first-time applicants from Great Britain and Northern Ireland. We are growing faster than giant kelp, ho, ho, ho!"

Viv nodded. "That's why the wait is so long: my friend had to wait for more than a year. But she says it was well worth it. An EU passport is a hot commodity these days. I wish I had an Irish granny."

"I can lend you mine, ho, ho, ho! You know that Nigel Farage applied for a German passport *one day* after the Brexit referendum. And he also got it for his kids: his wife is German. So they are all right. Other Brexiteers have also jumped on the EU bandwagon."

"But many ordinary people can't," reflected Viv.

"To be sure, to be sure."

"Proper mingin'," concluded Dali.

See, I've told you the youngster was bright, haven't I? Talking of which, I realised that the afternoon at the Grand Central Metropolitan presented me with an excellent opportunity for a quiet tête-à-tête with her: I didn't want anyone else overhearing us.

"May I have a word, Dali – in private?"

"Defo," agreed my young colleague, and we both moved away from the others. This wouldn't be easy, but, if I was going to make progress with her, there was no point in prevaricating. I started off – albeit somewhat haltingly – by assuring Dali that the way people spoke was a part of who they were and that nobody should feel bad about their accent or pronunciation.

My tutee appeared to be in total agreement. "Defo: you speak funny, li… you speak funny, but don' feel 'orrible: we're, lik… not gagged."

"You're not *gagged?*"

"No, no, we're not gagged 'cos we've 'eard worse."

"You've heard worse? You mean worse than *my accent?*"

"Defo," reassured me the girl with a consoling smile.

I must admit that it took me a little while to regain my composure, but, on reflection, Dali was only being honest. Actually, our politicians could take a leaf out of her book. To get my exposition back on track, I went rather over the top in expressing my gratitude for her reassurance before clarifying that I was actually taking about *her*. Looking back on it, I realise that I was rather rambling – I mean, it was such a sensitive thing to raise – but I explained that, rightly or wrongly, people did judge others on how they spoke and that, if she wanted to progress in her career, it might be an idea to listen carefully to her work colleagues and even to the BBC – I mean the British Broadcasting Corporation, *not* Bear's Buzzing Content – to get used to how things are pronounced in Standard English. To exemplify my points vis-à-vis dropping one's aitches, I mentioned her 'man Ant', 'armless' Theo and a few other apposite examples. While, initially, the girl was taken aback, she nevertheless listened carefully and agreed she would try.

Encouraged, I then tackled double negatives, although I started by saying that, inherently, there was nothing wrong with such constructions. Dali appeared pleased to learn that, in Polish and other Slavonic languages, double negatives were actually standard. But I did stress that English was a different language and that Standard English demanded single negatives. We then had some fun practising the aforementioned, and I must say that Dali did rather well. Actually, she did so well that, rather than terminating the lesson, I carried on, her ubiquitous question tag 'innit?' also requiring urgent attention. I was about to bring the session to a close but remembered the funny notice in our kitchenette. Perhaps we could inject some humour to the proceedings: it would be nice to end the lesson on a light-hearted note.

"You know the notice in our kitchenette, Dali? The one that says: *After the break, staff should empty the teapot and stand upside down on the draining board.*"

"Defo."

"Do you laugh when you see it?"

"Laugh? Why?"

"Because it says that it is *the staff* who should stand upside down on the draining board. But they meant *the teapot: the teapot* should be placed on the board."

Dali rested her chin on her hand, creased her forehead and sank deep into her thoughts. I let her digest my explanation for a while before naming this grammatical blunder.

"This error is called faulty coordination."

"What's coordination?"

"When we link words, phrases and clauses with the coordinating conjunctions *and, or* or *but*, for example: 'we must and will persevere', 'sink or swim', 'we are bloodied but unbowed' – constructions like this."

"So coordination is not 'ard – uhm, hard."

"Of course it isn't – we use it all the time. But as soon as you put a label on it, people panic and think, *It's grammar – I don't do grammar*. But the point is that we 'do' grammar every time we say or write something."

"Do we, li… do we really?"

"Absolutely. Because grammar is simply about how we arrange words so that they make sense."

"'S that *all?*"

"Well, there are lots and lots of principles organising language, and we need to be aware of them all. Coordination is just one of many grammatical categories. And, when you get it wrong, your message may get garbled. I will give you another example. I once read this in my local newspaper: 'A wheelie bin was found to be on fire in a passageway and was quickly put out.' What do you think was put out?"

"The bin?"

"No, what else could have been put out?"

"The fire?"

"Yes, of course, but they didn't actually say this. What do you think they should have written?"

The girl thought for a while before venturing: "And *the fire* were—"

"The fire *was*, Dali."

"And *the fire was* quickly put out?"

"Well done!"

The girl smiled, thought some more and, hesitating slightly, said: "Aston, he emailed us 'bout Dew; she phoned 'im… him."

"So what did his email say?"

"'Dew's granddad died and won't be in the office today'. But… but… it were… it was, li… the same mistake?"

I'm sure I don't have to tell you how impressed I was. "Bravo, bravo, Dali!"

"So, so, it should be… should be: 'and *she* won't be in the office today'?"

"What a clever young lady you are!"

***

After being released from our luxury detention, we trooped back to the now undoubtedly bug- and bomb-free office. It was already 4pm, but we were all working from home on the following day, which was Friday, as well as on the Monday after that, so we needed to sort out some stuff for our home-working. At least that's what Aston said.

"Our manifesto, our manifesto!" shouted Millie. "I finished it just before our meeting with Inco; I'll email it to you in a sec."

Soon, Millie's manifesto landed in our respective inboxes. It was entitled OUR DEMANDS. It went like this.

We, the employees at FART, are no longer willing to put up with outdated working practices, which neglect our Work-Life Balance and put our Wellbeing at risk. This is why WE DEMAND:

1. *Home-working to increase from two to AT LEAST THREE DAYS per week: Thursdays, Fridays and Mondays;*
2. *Bicycle-powered desks for all employees (unless they are permanently stationed in the Bahamas);*
3. *Additional space hoppers on each floor;*
4. *Challenging gender stereotyping;*
5. *Challenging micro-aggressions (eye-rolling, eye-narrowing, eyebrow-raising, tut-tutting, cheek-puffing, winking, folding one's arms, looking at the mobile phone);*
6. *Unconscious bias training;*
7. *Safe spaces for people to challenge their own biases and core character traits;*
8. *Designated TikTok time;*
9. *A day off to celebrate each of the following: Zero Discrimination Day, International Day for Biological Diversity, International Day of Happiness, World Mental Health Day and International Day of Potato;*
10. *Additional wellness programmes to include tickling therapy, stroking therapy and slapping therapy;*
11. *Title Mx to be used for those identifying as 'third sex';*
12. *Gender-neutral language;*
13. *Gender-neutral restrooms/facilities;*
14. *Unhappiness Leave;*
15. *Reinstating Secret Santa at FART's annual Christmas party.*

Millie Tant (she/her)
Secretary
EU

I was rather impressed by how comprehensive Millie's list was, although I was somewhat baffled by the Potato Day. Perhaps she had included it as a nod to Stu: my lovely hubby, who is also a Dubliner, had explained the special significance of this vegetable to his countrymen. Anyway, I was facing the next four days at home, Fridays and Mondays having been allocated to home-working, so I would be able to chew this over with him. What he wouldn't be able to help me with, though, was who Millie was actually working for. I mean, we had left the EU, so why was the block still employing her? Then again, Europe was supposed to be impossibly woke – that's what Brexiteers told us in 2016 anyway – so perhaps Ursula von der Leyen thought that Millie would make an ideal secretary? Clearly, the role was part-time, but we at FART did enjoy two office-free days, and, if the EU and Millie got their way, we would get another one. Come to think of it, could Millie actually be trying to destabilise our organisation from within at the behest of our erstwhile oppressor? A fifth column – that sort of thing. This required urgent clarification.

"Crystal, could Millie be a foreign agent, by any chance? Do you think she was this mole Inco wanted to flush out?"

When my Danish friend stopped laughing, she explained: "No, no, Millie's EU stands for 'Employees United'; it's our trade union."

"Oh, I s-e-e-e."

Much as I would have liked to discuss the merits and demerits of joining our trade union with Crystal, I was beckoned by Aston.

"This is for you, Ali. Make sure you read and digest everything. But no emails to me: I will be extremely busy. We'll touch base on Tuesday. Gotta shoot – toodle-oo."

With this, my mentor handed me a huge pile of papers. I wondered how on earth I was going to get it all home – I don't drive, and neither does my hubby – but needs must. Anyway, my biceps might benefit from a bit of weight training.

On Friday morning, I was in my home office before 9am: I didn't want my work colleagues to think that I was slacking – you never know: they might decide to check up on you at any time. I spread all Aston's papers on my desk and immersed myself in FART's policies, strategies, procedures, standards, visions, priorities, tenets, targets, agendas, initiatives, regulations, principles, doctrines, prescriptions, proscriptions, instructions, rules, precepts, commands, conventions, codes, protocols, directives, decrees, orders, schedules, exclusions, guidelines and recommendations. Oh, and process maps and process flow charts, of course.

Unfortunately, the very first document cautioned – in the strongest possible terms – against 'withholding the buy-in from key stakeholders deployed on the strategic AI deliverables in line with the governments topline initiatives in relation to enabling mechanisms, transactional signposts, predictors of beaconicity and knowledge bites'. While I no longer wondered how many governments they had in mind, having quickly twigged that using the apostrophe wasn't among my work colleagues' strengths, I couldn't make head or tail of the stuff. Given that the rest of the document wasn't much help either, I definitely needed assistance. Having waited until 9.30am to give Aston time to enjoy his black coffee with four sugars, I called him. I was, of course, mindful of the fact that he was going to be extremely busy, but what choice did I have? Regrettably, his answering machine informed me that he was on a conference call. Going through the events of the previous day in my mind, I couldn't recall any mentions of conference calls, but never mind: my enquiry would keep.

I thus put the document to one side and started on another. No sooner had I opened it than I hit another snag, for it was about 'the overarching focus of the stakeholder benchmarking transactional pathfinder consultation' which, apparently, was 'to interpret the implications of the governments AI vision and reach consensus through the Current Government Thinking Committee on what was required to secure their successful delivery'. I spent quite a while trying to work out how you could possibly deliver implications, but the report provided no explanation thereof. Given that the rest of it also failed to make any sense to me, I felt I had no option but to call Aston again. He couldn't possibly still be on his conference call: it had taken me ages to go through the entre shebang. Regrettably, his answering machine informed me that he was now on a Zoom call.

Essentially, this is how my home-working day unfolded: I kept being thwarted in my attempts to penetrate the impenetrable, and Aston's answering machine was doing its best to keep me at bay by informing me that my mentor was making excellent use of his allotted time for 'a personal appointment', which was followed by another three conference calls, two Zoom calls and some more of his 'protected time'. I'm sorry to report that, by the end of the working day, I had developed a thumping headache, which was accompanied by a motivational crisis. I was thus hugely relieved to have the entire weekend to recover. And I was beginning to appreciate the critical importance of our Wellness Department, with its allegedly helpful Molly Coddle and Val Erian. How on earth did Crystal manage to avoid any personal contact with them?

Mercifully, the weekend did restore my mental equilibrium, and I embarked on the following Monday's home-working with a renewed vigour. Tragically, the day proceeded in the same vein, although I had only enough stamina to withstand being advised of two conference calls, one Zoom call and one stretch of 'protected time' of Aston's. By 3.30pm, I'd had enough, so I instructed my answering machine to announce to the world at large that I was on my very own conference call and went for a walk to clear my head.

8

Multiple Visions, Solutions-Driven Agendas and the Singapore Takeaway

I never thought I would be as relieved as I was when I got to the office on Tuesday, although I dreaded Aston's inquisition into my grasp of FART's policies, strategies, procedures, etc, etc, etc. Not to mention process maps and process flow charts.

The day, however, started on an uncontroversial note, my mentor enquiring: "Good weekend, I take it?"

"It was, Aston, thank you."

"And two productive working days?"

"Uhmm... uhhh... erm... I... I didn't quite..."

Thankfully, Aston didn't seem particularly interested in my two productive working days, announcing: "Mine were frantically busy – *frantically*. One can be infinitely more productive when one works from home – *infinitely* – you know what I'm saying."

"Naturally, Aston, naturally."

"Anyways, you are in luck: the CID are going to sort you out today. Mrs Ana Chronic is retiring tomorrow, but she has kindly agreed to take you on, right? She is very experienced so will be able to answer any questions you might have. But it should now all be clear: you had two days to get to grips with the stuff I gave you on Thursday. Good timing, right?"

"Very, very good!" I enthusiastically agreed, hoping that my session with Mrs Chronic might help me to gloss over my comprehensive comprehension fiasco.

"But it will be her very last induction training, so go easy on her, huh, huh, huh!"

"I will, I will, Aston!"

As was customary, we started the day with our cluster huddle, which seemed even more intimate than last week's. It must have been the result of our four-day separation. And they say that technology can replace human contact; perhaps Dali and Dew should be told. Aston then went off to some meeting, and I tried to get to grips with more bumf before making for Aberdeen. No, not in Scotland – on the twenty-seventh floor.

The silver-haired CID lady greeted me with a welcoming, "Lovely to meet you; I'm Ana."

"Lovely to meet you too; I'm Ali."

"Aston told me he'd made an excellent start on mentoring you."

"Yes, yes, excellent, *very* excellent."

"Did he tell you about our rebranding, pet?"

"Well, he said that… that we had been repurposed. By the Tories. Before they were kicked out."

"Yes, pet; they were trying their best."

"And also that our title had been changed. From regulation to radicalisation. And that we needed to keep it as vague as possible."

"Yes, Aston is excellent; you are in very capable hands, pet."

"I know, I know."

"But we now have a new government. New-ish, anyway. So we will have to rebrand again."

"Really? Why?"

"Because this is how it works, pet. When a new government comes in, things always change. By definition. A new broom sweeps clean. Look at Trump."

"Do you think our government is modelling itself on the Trump administration?"

"Well, they are all very complimentary about it, aren't they, pet? And are quickly retracting what they said in the past. Look at David Lammy and Peter Mandelson."

"Hmmm…"

"So we will shortly be launching a stakeholder benchmarking transactional pathfinder consultation, pet."

"Wow; it's sounds very… very transactional. Aston did say you had to be transactional. Like Trump."

"Yes, Aston is excellent; you are in very capable hands, pet. We've commissioned the dunce to handle our corporate rebranding exercise."

"*But why?*"

"To make sure we get outstanding quality."

"Can you get outstanding quality from *a dunce?*"

"No, no, no, not a dunce – *the* dunce. We've commissioned the very best in the industry. Have you not heard of *the dunce*, pet?"

"Well, I have definitely come across quite a few of them, but…"

"You can't have, pet: they are unique."

"I'm sorry but I'm not with you, Ana."

"If you want a stunning corporate identity, pet, you commission the Delivery of Unique Names for Corporations and Enterprises; they are superb."

"Oh, I s-e-e-e-e, DUNCE."

"That's what I've said, pet. And when our stakeholder benchmarking transactional pathfinder consultation reports, we'll roll out our new corporate identity."

"Does it roll?"

"It usually does, pet."

"Can't wait. But… but you… but we… we seem to use rather a lot of acronyms, don't we?"

"Doesn't everybody, pet?" Ana seemed genuinely puzzled by my intimation that the quantity of acronyms used by FART might be anything other than perfectly normal. "You must remember that we are a cutting-edge, forward-looking and progressive organisation."

"Yes, yes, I've noticed."

"That's why we have a relatively flat management structure, by the way."

"*Flat?* It… it doesn't strike me as *particularly* flat."

"Everything is relative, pet: you want to see the structure of piss."

"*I beg your pardon?*"

"The structure of the Pre-eminent Institute for Supersizing Strategies is much less straightforward. They are our partner organisation."

"Oh, PISS, ha, ha, ha – silly me! You mean

supersizing like in portion sizes in the States?"

"No, no, it has nothing to do with portion sizes in the States."

"So how does one supersize strategies?"

"The best way is to publish a position paper entitled *Supersizing Strategies*, pet; I understand it works really well. Anyway, let's concentrate on FART. You will be aware that every organisation in the public sector needs a Corporate Mission, won't you?"

"Absolutely, you can't do without one – not in the public sector."

"You can't, pet. Did Aston tell you about our Corporate Mission?"

"Hmm… arrr… radicalising… radicalising AI blueprints… I mean inherent innovative capacities?"

"Not quite, pet, not quite: it's one of our Overarching Corporate Objectives – but not our Corporate Mission."

"No, no, of course not – it couldn't possibly be."

"No. So what do you think it may be?"

"It's… it's… it's… it may be…"

"To keep our jobs, pet."

"Yes, yes, of course; Aston did tell me that!"

"Yes, Aston is excellent; you are in very capable hands, pet. But a Corporate Mission is not enough."

"No way, no way – it couldn't possibly be."

"No. So what else would you need, pet?"

"A government grant?"

"That as well, pet, but you also need a vision."

"Goes without saying; a vision will be absolutely necessary – *absolutely*."

"It will, pet, it will. Actually, we have multiple visions."

"*Multiple* visions? You mean like in 2016, when our Brexity politicians had all these visions of sunlit uplands, bespoke free-trade deals with Donald Trump and world-wide dominance?"

"Similar, similar." Ana turned around and pointed at two large signs hanging on the opposite wall. The signs read:

From Radicalisation of Transformation to Economic Miracle

Policy Makes Perfect

"But I thought it was practice – *practice* makes perfect?"

"A-a-a-a, but what comes before practice, pet?"

"Hmm… what comes before practice?"

"Policy, of course."

"Of course, of course – it always does!"

"Yes. And, as far as our sponsoring government department is concerned, the more policies, the better."

"Naturally – goes without saying."

"It does, pet, it does. And aims, targets, goals and objectives – they are also awfully important. Without aims, targets, goals and objectives, you can forget about the economic miracle."

"Yes, yes, just forget it."

"Unfortunately, we can't, pet. Unless we engineer an economic miracle, the government is screwed. They've said on the BBC that Trump wants Britain to increase defence spending to 5% of our national income. That would be billions more each year."

"Yes, yes, I've heard. Quite a jump from our current 2.3%. But Poland spends over 4%, so it can be done."

"Maybe, but I think Trump is asking too much, pet."

"Hmm, yes, he was supposed to be on our side."

"He was, he was, pet."

"But when he sees weakness in you, he will walk all over you. And Britain has isolated itself from the rest of Europe. That's why he loves Brexit. He and Putin both."

Ana nodded in agreement before restoring order to the proceedings: "Returning to our aims, targets, goals and objectives, pet, did Aston tell you about them?"

"Uhm… not in so many words."

"Well then, pet, we have the Collective Goals for Cluster and Sectional Operational Teams. They, of course, contribute to the fulfilment of our Divisional Operating Goals, which themselves feed into the Operational Development Targets for the Department. They – in turn – always progress to the Overarching Directorate Aims, which lead to the Cross-cutting Strategic Objectives, which, of course, feed into FART's Corporate Development Plan."

"That's… that's very reassuring."

"It is, pet. We also have Strategic Priorities, Key Management Targets and Overarching Corporate Objectives."

"Wow, I don't think we need to worry about the economic miracle – not with all those aims, targets, goals and objectives."

"No, we don't, pet; it's only a matter of time."

"Dead cert, Ana, dead cert. But I thought you'd said we had multiple visions – are there any others?"

"There are, pet: we also have a shared vision."

"Which is?"

"A vision which is shared."

"Really? But with whom?"

"What do you mean *with whom*, pet?"

"If it's a shared vision, it's presumably shared *with* somebody, isn't it?"

"Well, we haven't thought about it like this, pet, to be honest."

"Maybe with our sponsoring government department? And PISS perhaps?"

"Perhaps. We also have a common purpose," continued Ana.

"Which is?"

"A purpose which is common, pet."

"Really? And this purpose is...?"

"To replace teachers with AI. But we can't talk about this openly. Not yet anyway."

"Yes, yes, both Aston and Inco did say. We even have to sleep in separate bedrooms."

"But Aston and Inco are both married, pet."

"No, no, I didn't mean not sleeping with *them*... I meant not sleeping with your *husband*... no, no, I didn't mean *your* husband... I meant..."

"My husband is dead, pet."

"Oh, I'm awfully sorry, Ana."

"Thank you, pet. But that's not all."

"It isn't? Who else is dead?"

"No, no, nobody else is dead: we also have an agenda for action."

Phew, this saved me from further embarrassment, and I eagerly enquired: "Which is...?"

"Solutions-driven, of course."

"Of course, of course; no point having an agenda that isn't solutions-driven – no point at all."

"No," agreed Ana with a confirmatory nod.

"But... but what exactly are these solutions?"

"Getting it right first time, pet. We've been doing this ever since I can remember; it was covered in the very first induction I delivered – over forty years ago."

"But, if we've been getting it right first time for the past forty years, how come we need those constant changes?"

"Hmm, we haven't thought about this, pet, to be honest. But, if the government wants you to change things, you change things. Otherwise, you won't get your government grant."

"No, no, I mean yes – naturally."

"Now, what do you think we have to do to make sure we deliver our mission, visions, common purpose and agenda for action, pet?"

"Hmm... perhaps... maybe... what exactly do we have to do?"

"Embrace change, pet."

"But... but Aston said we harnessed it."

"A-a-a-a, but what do you have to do *before* you can harness change, pet?"

"Hmm, what do you have to do before you can harness change?"

"You have to *embrace* it, pet."

"Of course, of course: how else could we harness it?"

"We couldn't, pet. And our committees are instrumental there. Do you know about our committees?"

"Well, Aston and Crystal said that we did lots of meetings. Do they involve committees?"

"They certainly do, pet."

"Do we have plenty?"

"No more than other public-sector organisations, pet. Let me show you."

Ana bent over her laptop and projected a slide onto the screen. The slide read:

FART'S COMMITTEES – SLIDE ONE

- *Committee for the Resounding Approval of Policies (CRAP)*
- *Committee for the Operational Reviews of Processes, Strategies and Endorsements (CORPSE)*
- *Corporate Mission Committee*
- *Shared Vision Committee*
- *Common Purpose Committee*
- *Agenda for Action Committee*
- *Transformational Policy Committee*
- *Current Government Thinking Committee*
- *Ministerial Priorities Committee*
- *Radicalisation Committee*
- *AI Committee*
- *Joint Committee*
- *Disjointed Committee*
- *Ad Hoc Committee*
- *Post Hoc Committee*
- *House, Lift and Stairwell Committee*

"Wow; that's a lot of committees, Ana. But it's a bit unclear: is it a transformational policy or a transformational committee?"

"All our policies are transformational, pet."

"In that case, I think it might be clearer if you used a hyphen."

"*A hyphen?*"

"Yes: you'd write Transformational-Policy Committee – with the hyphen between transformational and policy."

"I don't think we use hyphens here, pet; not as a rule."

"So I gather, so I gather. But they really help."

"Do they, pet?"

"Absolutely. Compare 'a little used car' – without the hyphen – with 'a little-used car' – with the hyphen. Or 'a black cab driver' with 'a black-cab driver'. There are lots of phrases which are funny without the hyphen."

"*Funny*, pet?"

"Absolutely; for example, 'a hard drug user', 'a used car salesman', 'a dirty joke teller', 'a stuffed mushroom lover' – lots and lots."

"Hmm, I'm not sure what a stuffed lover has to do with our committees, pet."

"But it's not a stuffed *lover* – it's a stuffed *mushroom*. That's exactly why you need the hyphen there."

"This may well be so, pet, but nothing will change without an approval by CRAP."

"I see. They must be very influential."

"They are, pet, they are. Where were we?"

"Hyphens."

"No, no, before the hyphens."

"Our committees."

"Oh yes." Ana bent over her laptop again and projected a second slide, which read:

FART'S COMMITTEES – CONTINUED (2)

- *Navigating Assembly*
- *Overall Direction Steering Group*
- *Overall Information Strategy Advisory Group*
- *Overarching Internal Communications Task Group*
- *Overarching External Communications Task Group*
- *Digital Technology Implementation Committee*
- *Digital Technology User's Taskforce*
- *Digital Technology Advisory Forum*
- *Enabling Stakeholder Liaison and Monitoring Group*
- *External Customer's Working Group*
- *External Working Customer's Group*

"Wow! I had no idea any organisation could have so many committees."

"So you can't have worked in the public sector before, pet."

"No, I haven't, Ana. FART is… is quite an eye-opener."

"Yes, we do things properly here."

"I'm sure you… we do, I'm sure we do."

"But *even here*, not everything is perfect, pet. Take the Navigating Assembly and the Overall Direction Steering Group, for example."

"In what way aren't they perfect?"

"Well, they *themselves* may be perfect, but the problem is that they don't often pull in the same direction."

"Oh dear, that's not very good, is it? Not if they are supposed to navigate and steer."

"It isn't, pet, it isn't. But when the planetary conditions are favourable, they do come together. It is then that we get truly spectacular results."

"And how often are the planetary conditions favourable?"

"Unfortunately, not very often, pet. But we have marvellous examples of cooperation – *marvellous*. For example, the Overall Information Strategy Advisory Group has been recently formed as a result of a rather harmonious merger between the Overall Information Advisory Group and the Overall Strategy Advisory Group."

"I'm delighted it was harmonious."

"So is everybody else, pet. They've been carrying out some groundbreaking work recently."

"Oh yes?"

"They've come up with a coherent, cohesive, cogent and cognisable information strategy."

"Wow! Such a strategy can't fail, surely."

"No, it can't, pet. Did Aston explain about the central plank of this strategy?"

"Uhmm… no, he didn't."

"Well, the *central* plank of our coherent, cohesive, cogent and cognisable information strategy is that *information has to be about something.*"

"Wow – unbelievable!"

"That's why they are developing our information architecture – to support the strategy. Inco is working up the finer detail."

"Inco Herent?"

"No, no, Inco Municado. I won't be here – I'm retiring tomorrow – but all the other colleagues are looking forward to the roll-out."

"I can imagine, I can imagine: rolling architecture must be quite a sight. By the way, I hope you will have a long and fulfilling retirement, Ana."

"Thank you, pet. But I haven't finished yet. As far as the Overarching Internal Communications Task Group is concerned, there have been many discussions as to whether it should be primarily concerned with overarching tasks or whether it should be overarching itself. But the issue hasn't been resolved yet. As far as I know, they would prefer the latter."

"And who could blame them? *Overarching group* sounds much better."

"It does, pet, it does. I think they've been discussing this since 1997. But they are hoping for a resolution by Christmas."

"A resolution would be good. Particularly by Christmas."

"It would, pet. But they are incredibly consistent – for years and years, they have been passing a resolution that internal communications ought to be improved."

"And have internal communications improved?"

"Well, they keep passing this resolution, so I imagine there is still some way to go, pet."

"Internal communications can be tricky at the best of times."

"They can, pet, they can. Anyway, let's move on: the Digital Technology Implementation Committee collaborates very closely with the Digital Technology

User's Taskforce. But, unfortunately, it struggles to forge a constructive working relationship with the Digital Technology Advisory Forum."

"What an awful shame."

"It is, pet, it is."

"But, Ana, was it worth mobilising a taskforce for one solitary digital technology user?"

"*One* user? We have many digital technology users, pet."

"Not according to the name of this taskforce."

"I'm not with you, pet."

"You have the apostrophe after 'user'."

"Because it's about possession, pet."

"But the apostrophe needs to go after the plural 'users'."

"Are you sure, pet?"

"Cross my heart and hope to die. The same goes for customers: I presume you have more than one customer in each group?"

"We have lots of them, pet."

"So you need the apostrophe after 'customers'."

Ana looked at me quizzically. "I suppose you could escalate this to CRAP. But, unfortunately, our External Customer's Working Group tends to be confused with our External Working Customer's Group."

"Can't say I'm surprised, Ana. And I think those misplaced apostrophes only add to the confusion."

"Hmm, do they really? Anyway, our *working* customers are too busy working to attend many meetings, so this Group doesn't convene all that often. But our *external* customers – they are really keen. They want to meet virtually all the time. In fact, we have started wondering whether it might be our working lunches."

"Can't say I'm surprised, Ana. This banquet we had at the Grand Central Metropolitan – do all our committees get such feasts?"

"They do, pet, they do."

"In that case, this might warrant a little investigation."

"That's what we all thought. Anyway, we have a few more committees."

On the third slide, I could see:

FART'S COMMITTEES – CONTINUED (3)

- *Cerebral Forum*
- *Editorial Forum*
- *Blue Sky Thinking Executive*
- *Customer Focus Taskforce*
- *Marketing and Market Penetration Issues Focus Group*
- *Invention Taskforce*
- *Speculation Squad*
- *Execution Gang*
- *Intra-Organisational Cluster*
- *Inter-Divisional Liaison Group*

"Wow, I… I don't know what to say, Ana."

"You are not the only one, pet."

"But… but why exactly is this Executive blue?"

"No, no, no, what's blue is *the sky*."

"In *this* country?"

"It's not about the sky in this country, pet – it's about thinking."

"Well, hyphens would *definitely* help there: Blue-Sky-Thinking Executive."

"Hmm, you could try escalating this to CRAP, I suppose. But I must tell you about the Cerebral Forum and the Editorial Forum: there is an intense animosity between them."

"Is there really?"

"Yes, regrettably. The Editorial Forum feel quite strongly that they should be merged with the Cerebral Forum."

"But why?"

"To form the Cerebral Editorial Forum. They say that the existence of these two separate forums gives the general impression that the editors are not cerebral."

"Actually, Ana, from what I've heard about Ignor Amus and Phillis Tine..."

"But the Cerebral Forum won't entertain such a merger: they are very protective of their cerebral remit. Between you and me, pet, they look down on the Editorial Forum. It's a very unsatisfactory situation."

"Yes, yes, it does seem very unsatisfactory, Ana, although..."

"On the positive side, our Customer Focus Taskforce have literally surpassed themselves."

"We have *Customer Focus Taskforce as well?*"

"We have, we have, pet. They have embraced customer focus with real gusto."

"Actually, Chardonnay did say that we prided ourselves on delivering customer focus."

"We do, we do, pet. And the Taskforce are delivering customer focus quite relentlessly."

"Do you think they get tired?"

"They must do, pet. Still, they stay incredibly focused. I have another slide for you here, pet."

Ana projected the slide, which read:

THE CUSTOMER FOCUS TASKFORCE

- *Embraces Customer Focus*
- *Delivers Customer Focus*
- *Relentlessly Focuses on:*
  - *Customer Satisfaction*
  - *Customer Journey*
  - *Customer Experience*
  - *Customer Relationships*
  - *Customer Demands*
  - *Customer Views*
  - *Customer Insights*
  - *Customer Judgements*
  - *Customer Gratification*
  - *Customer Fulfilment*
  - *Customer Engagement*
  - *Customer Empowerment*
  - *Customer Touchpoints*
  - *Customer Flashpoints*
  - *Customer Enhancement*

"Wow, that's… that's quite extraordinary."

"It certainly is, pet."

"I mean, with all these committees, assemblies, executives, taskforces, fora, squads, gangs and gr…"

At that moment, there was a knock on the door.

"That will be the lunch," said Ana.

"Good afternoon. I've got your lunch," said the lunch gentleman, wheeling in a trolley full of trays and plates sitting alongside a few vessels.

"Good afternoon, Frank; thank you very much. Ali, this is Frank Furter. He heads our Catering Department. Frank, this is Ali. She's just joined us."

"Pleased to meet you, Frank. Your lunches are simply… are out of this world."

"Thank you, Ali. We do our best; you can't let colleagues waste away, can you? We'll fatten you up in no time."

"Is Victoria off today?" enquired Ana.

"No, no, but I wanted to say goodbye in person."

"That's very kind, Frank; I'll miss your lunches. Forty years' worth of them." Ana dabbed her eyes with a tissue as she embraced Frank.

After he had gone, I looked at the trolley: the offering was exactly the same as that which Aston and I had received in Nairn.

Ana and I were halfway through our lunch when the door opened and in strode Inco Herent wearing the executive look I vividly remembered from our previous encounter.

"Hiya, guys! Oh, lunch – what a nice surprise."

Our unexpected visitor – or perhaps, to Ana, he wasn't *entirely* unexpected – didn't waste any time on pleasantries (he didn't even acknowledge me) and got stuck right in. When he finished, he swept the contents of several trays into his doggy bag and, with a brief, "Adios," was gone.

Ana looked at me with a smile. "We'd better call it a day, pet; we covered a lot of ground this morning. I wouldn't want you to get overwhelmed. I'm sure Aston will fill any remaining gaps; you are in good hands. Good luck with your job."

"Thank you ever so much, Ana; have a great retirement."

When I returned to my workstation, I found most colleagues hard at whatever they needed to be hard at. Before, however, I had the chance to look at another pile of papers someone had dumped on my desk, Aston announced to the entire cluster: "The Singapore takeaway is off."

Just as well that I've just had my lunch, I thought. The message was nevertheless worrying.

"Oh dear, I hope nobody has got sick, Aston."

"Sick of *what*, Ali?"

"Well, not *of* what – *with* what: if it's off, it will make people sick."

"Steady on, steady on, we are not *that* dedicated, you know what I'm saying."

"But I understand that it is popular with colleagues."

"Fairly popular, yes."

"So a lot of people will get sick."

"Why would people get sick?"

"E. coli, salmonella, listeria, botulism, things like that."

"*What are you on about, Ali?*"

"Food poisoning, what else? This Singapore takeaway round the corner, *The Merlion*. I've always suspected—"

"No, no, no: I meant the lessons from Nota's fact-finding mission to Singapore. We were going to attend *the Foremost Forum* this afternoon to listen to her findings, right?"

"Oh, I s-e-e-e-e. But why is this takeaway off?"

"Because air traffic controllers are working from home today, you know what I'm saying."

"Well, these days everybody else works from home at least a few days a week, so they probably didn't want to be left out. And who can blame them, Aston?"

"But this practically closed the airspace above Britain, so Nota is still in the air, right?"

"Probably circling somewhere above the Caspian Sea, ho, ho, ho!" Stu threw his head back as he laughed.

"Aye, aye, pish," announced Jock. He was normally very quiet, so it was nice that he felt able to contribute – although I had no idea what 'pish' actually meant.

"But why did she have to go all the way to Singapore?"

Theo, who must have been listening, was quick with an explanation: "Because we are a research and development hub." The pride in his voice was unmistakable. "That's why James Dyson buggered off to Singapore."

"He was one of the key proponents of Brexit," added Crystal. "Many millionaires and billionaires were. Because they knew that Brexit would make them even richer."

"Unlike the rest of us?" enquired Dew.

"Unlike the rest of us, Dew."

"Proper mingin'," reflected Dali.

Theo appeared to be in his element. "Dyson moved his company to Singapore in 2019. And, last year, he cut nearly a third of his UK workforce. That's 1,000 British jobs gone. He said that Britain lacked engineering talent."

"So much for 'made in Britain'! He used to pretend that he cared about British manufacturing." Viv shook her head in apparent disgust.

Crystal executed a deep nod. "Yep, and now hiring workers from the EU costs much more and is more complicated than before Brexit. So he cleared off to Asia."

"As I've said, self-interest always wins. And greed. Particularly if you are very rich, right?" reflected Aston.

"That's *precisely why* you are very rich." Ant definitely had a point there.

Theo seemed to have an impressive grasp of the relevant facts and figures: "Dyson may be self-serving, but he isn't stupid: we… I mean Singapore has a lot going for it – it excels at education, for example. Its PISA results for 2022 put it in the first place internationally. And, in 2024, its economy grew by 2.7% and productivity by 1.7%. And here, they are stagnant."

I wasn't surprised. "We don't have enough workers for a start. That's probably why FART has employed me."

"Probably, Ali," agreed Aston.

"Apparently, Britain is the only G7 country with the workforce smaller than before the Covid pandemic. There are now 800,000 more economically inactive people than in 2020. Brexit hasn't helped, of course," said Viv with a pensive nod.

"Listen, listen, we shouldn't really be using the 'B' word," cautioned Aston, looking around somewhat nervously.

"Why not?"

"Because our current government hasn't grown any balls, ho, ho, ho!" interjected Stu. "All the right-wingers keep accusing it of trying to reverse Brexit, so it's petrified."

"But the majority of people now agree that Brexit was the greatest act of economic self-sabotage ever," added Ant, who had been quiet so far.

Crystal laughed. "But the government haven't yet received the feedback from their strategic and far-ranging inquiry focus groups."

"Are there strategic and far-ranging inquiry focus groups, Crystal?"

"You bet! But it may take years before they report back, Ali."

"Why years?" asked Dew.

"Inquiries usually take years, Dew. Not in other countries – they are much quicker there – I mean in Britain. Look at the infected-blood-scandal inquiry. Or the Chilcot report into intelligence failures in Iraq. The Covid-19 inquiry is also likely to take several years."

"Proper mingin.'" I will let you guess who said this.

Stu chortled again. "To be sure. So our rulers are waiting for their strategic and far-ranging inquiry focus groups to tell them how they should feel about Brexit."

Aston gave a grave nod. "But, until then, we aren't supposed to utter the 'B' word. It's on the list of proscribed words and phrases. You know we have a list of proscribed words and phrases, Ali, don't you?"

"Actually, I didn't; do we really?"

Crystal laughed. "It includes 'Minister for Brexit Opportunities'. Boris Johnson created the post in 2020, but it was abolished in 2022, and we aren't allowed to mention it."

Stu's laughter echoed Crystal's. "Can't think why. After all, Britain is now free to trade with the likes of Afghanistan, Angola and Bangladesh. What an incredible opportunity, ho, ho, ho!"

"Yes, Johnson has a lot to answer for," reflected Viv.

Jock nodded in apparent agreement. "Aye, aye, bampot." While Jock's 'bampot' remained unexplained, at least his nod offered a clue.

"But… but many people voted for Boris Johnson in 2019, didn't they?" enquired Dew. "I was too young, but my parents told me."

"Look, Dew, if you feel neglected and left behind and this bloke with ruffled hair comes along and promises you the earth – oven-ready everything, world dominance in everything and sunlit uplands everywhere – why wouldn't you vote for him? Particularly if he says he has a tiger in his tank, dangles from a zip wire for you and, like this geezer in the pub, fails to tuck his shirt into his trousers properly? A regular bloke. Or so he wants you to believe."

It was clear that Crystal was on the same page as me.

"Careful, careful here," cautioned us Aston. "Some people still think Johnson is bee's knees, cat's whiskers, ant's pants and all the rest of it."

"I didn't know ants had pants, Aston."

"It's just a saying, Ali."

"Sorry, I meant it as a joke."

"Talking of ant jokes," interjected Stu, "why don't ants get Covid?"

"Why don't ants get Covid, Stu?"

"Because they have anty bodies, ho, ho, ho! How can you tell male ants from female ants?"

"How, Stu?"

"They are all female; otherwise, they would be called uncles. What will happen if an ant gets silenced?"

"What will 'appen – happen – if an ant gets silenced?" asked Dali.

"It will become a mutant, ho, ho, ho!"

9

Demigods, Hallucinations and Work-Life Balance of Refuse Collectors

The following few weeks passed in a flurry of activity: blue-sky-thinking executives, multiple visions, cross-cutting strategic objectives, speculation squads, solutions-driven agendas, implementation gangs, transactional signposts, execution gangs, enabling stakeholder liaisons, navigating assemblies – stuff along those lines. Not to mention plenty of intimate cluster huddles and sumptuous lunches – both in our offices and at the Grand Central Metropolitan.

But that morning was different. All the ladies on our floor seemed particularly agitated, and, when I went to the loo after our cluster huddle, I practically had to fight my way to the sink: in front of every single mirror there were at least three female colleagues applying lipstick, reapplying their mascara, powdering their nose and combing their hair – something was definitely afoot. You will undoubtedly be pleased to learn that, before returning to my desk, I did manage to wash my hands.

No sooner had I resumed my position than I heard what sounded like a collective gasp: "Rushdi's coming, Rushdi's coming!"

I looked round and saw a new gentleman entering our office. And, in that instant, I understood. Rushdi was very tall, very dark and very handsome. Wow. I mean, don't get me wrong, I'm too old for that sort of thing, but one is supposed to go weak in the presence of beauty, isn't one? At least that's what the well-known song says. Rushdi seemed well aware of the impact his entrance had made on the female segment of the staff – I imagine this would happen every single time he put in an appearance, so he would be accustomed to it. Having halted his progress right at the centre of the room, he tilted his head ever so slightly and nonchalantly flicked an imaginary strand of hair away from his face: his jet-black braids were arranged far too tightly to allow any strands to break free.

At that moment, we heard a loud thud. When we turned towards its source, we saw Millie jumping up from her desk and, in the process, dislodging a pile of thick files, which were falling onto the floor in a small avalanche.

"Please, please, sit down, sit down, Rushdi; can I get you a coffee? Or something?"

You see, Rushdi didn't have his own desk in our office. I mean, he worked from home, didn't he? After he took possession of Millie's speedily vacated desk, he was surrounded by an adoring coven.

"Lovely to see you, Rushdi; how are you?"

"Tired: I had to get up at 7.45am."

"How absolutely awful!"

Rushdi nodded and looked at Millie, who was gazing at him expectantly, her torso leaning towards him at a slightly unnatural angle.

"Milky coffee please, Millie; no sugar. I'm sweet enough, ha, ha, ha!"

The smitten ladies echoed Rushdi enthusiastically, and Millie sprinted for the door. What was that about challenging gender stereotyping she had demanded in her manifesto? I couldn't help reaching the conclusion that I had just witnessed a stark manifestation of how biology trumps ideology – if ever there was one.

"I wouldn't bother, Millie: we are going to the Grand Central Metropolitan. There will be refreshments there. And then lunch." This came from Aston, whose reflexes, however, didn't quite match Millie's, for she was already gone.

What quickly transpired was that Rushdi, who, as Crystal had earlier explained, was the only employee with genuine AI expertise our organisation had to its name, was going to present us with the findings of his painstaking research into the wonders of this groundbreaking technology. This is why we needed to go to the Grand Central Metropolitan: our office building didn't have meeting rooms sufficiently large to accommodate the entire staff.

Soon, we could be seen retracing our steps to the hotel, with which I was already familiar – I mean both the steps and the hotel. In the spacious lobby, we were greeted by a row of tables groaning under the weight of Danish pastries, croissants, jam-smothered pancakes, muffins, doughnuts, coconut cakes, biscuits and fruit and a mind-bogglingly wide assortment of toasted sandwiches on both brown and white. I could see that, to wash it all down, we had tea, coffee, hot chocolate, mineral water – both still and sparkling – and an assortment of fruit juices.

"Have a coconut cake, Rushdi!" exclaimed Millie obsequiously. "It's absolutely delicious."

I wondered if the prohibition on using the 'C' word had now been lifted, but this was neither the time nor the place to pursue the matter with Millie, who was wrapping herself round Rushdi rather tightly. Having enjoyed the sumptuous refreshments at a pleasingly relaxed pace, we were called to order by Aston, who started clapping loudly while announcing: "Nota's here, Nota's here; let's go in."

"Air-traffic controllers must be back in their towers." Although it had been a while since Nota's unfortunate travel incident, Stu's remark made me giggle at the memory of the surreal episode. Surreal maybe, but you never know with this working-from-home lark, do you?

We all entered the conference room, our cluster taking possession of the middle row – as per usual.

Once we were all seated, Nota, enveloped in the air of authority, stood on the podium, with Inco taking a seat right next to it.

"Morning, troops, and welcome to this important, significant and momentous digital-technology strategic direction forum, at which our AI expert, Rushdi, will present the findings of his meticulous research into the groundbreaking potential of this revolutionary technology. You are undoubtedly cognizant that our core values are openness, transparency, leadership and digital. To those who think that digital is not a value, I say: digital revolutionises everything."

"*Radicalises*," hissed Inco. I wondered if he felt disgruntled that it wasn't he who was standing on the podium instead of her. I was also a little disappointed that Ana hadn't mentioned our core values during my CID induction.

"You are also doubtless cognizant that our previous government, which inspirationally created the Government Digital Service, entrusted us with the visionary mission to revolutionise—"

"To *radicalise*," hissed Inco again.

"To *radicalise* education in this country by embracing AI, and—"

"By *tightening our grip* on AI." I'm sure you can guess who said this. I mean hissed.

"And our current government is *even more* digitally capable…"

Tell this to the HMRC people, I thought.

"…and it wants us to mainline AI into the veins of—"

"Into the *arteries*."

"To mainline AI into the *arteries* of education, so Rushdi's expert insights will be invaluable. Rushdi, please."

The demigod took Nota's place and immediately launched into his learned exposition, which prevented me from pondering if education actually had arteries. Or, for that matter, veins.

"Artificial Intelligence is superior machine intelligence exhibited by complex computer systems that enable digital tools to form an extraordinary perception of their environment and use learning and intelligence to create sophisticated models capable of taking appropriate actions to maximise their chances of achieving a wide range of pre-defined goals and objectives such as ratiocination, knowledge representation, blueprinting, apprehending, natural language processing, perceptiveness and scaffolding for robotics that are going to shape all our futures in most groundbreaking ways which will revolutionise – and *radicalise* – all spheres of human activity."

It pains me to admit this, but I was lost already. And, if I'm being honest, being distracted by his beauty didn't help either. I nevertheless resolved to pay as much attention as I could possibly muster: we might not see him for another month – or even longer. His words would wash over me like crashing waves, which would then quickly recede – at least in my tiny brain. How could a layperson possibly grasp the intricacies of this ratiocinating technology?

Rushdi went on about transcendental possibilities and emergent abilities of AI, which, apparently, would shift our mindset. I couldn't help wondering if I was included among those whose mindset would be shifted. And if I was, what if I didn't like it? Was this shift even reversible? But, again, there was no opportunity to ponder this existential conundrum, for Rushdi was in full flow. He said that AI had a thingy akin to a brain which was, apparently, tuned by something called the optimalisation algorithm and demanded tons of data to be trained on. I wondered if we had entered the age when even machines were making demands on us. Unfortunately, Rushdi got me lost again with his elaboration of platforms and systems that are AI enabled and domain-specific versions of AI models. But then, he said something about education, so I tuned in with a renewed determination to comprehend.

Apparently, in education we needed personalised adaptive systems – whatever they were. And there was me thinking that, in education, we needed highly competent and well-paid teachers. But maybe this was the problem: producing highly competent teachers and paying them well was awfully expensive, and Trump wanted us to increase our defence spending to 5%. And didn't seem too keen on giving us this bespoke free-trade deal promised by our political visionaries in 2016 either.

Rushdi then talked about some obscure mathematical process called backpropagation pattern recognition and deep-learning technique, or were they processes – in the plural? I was now getting desperate, but there was more: apparently – in this process, or were they processes? – something called matrix multiplications were used during training to extract patterns from large datasets. He said that this extraction was actually how this AI learnt – who would have thought? And did you know that matrix multiplications had something to do with linear algebra? No, me neither: I'm a linguist – not a mathematician. What is linear algebra, by the way?

Suddenly, I heard a loud snore on my left. I turned and saw Aston, who was positioned next to me, slumped in his seat. Although I wasn't exactly sure what the protocol for arousing one's mentor from their slumber was, I hoped that a gentle nudge wouldn't be inappropriate. Having been jolted out of his snooze, Aston sat bolt upright and declared: "Illuminating, most illuminating, you know what I'm saying." After enthusiastically agreeing, I surveyed the hall. The female contingent was soaking up Rushdi's words with a beatific expression on its collective face, whereas the guys were... what exactly *were* they doing? Praying? Each had his head bowed quite low, after all. It didn't, however, take me long to realise that they were simply fiddling with their mobile phones, which were nestling on their respective laps. Then again, the modern obsession with smart mobile devices doesn't seem too dissimilar from religion – at least not in terms of its fervour. I'm largely impervious, by the way, but then I'm a self-confessed dinosaur. And I was rather glad that Millie appeared to be seized by ecstasy, because it clearly made her oblivious to this act of micro-aggression now being apparently perpetrated by the male audience. Do you remember her manifesto? The one in which she listed looking at one's mobile phone while in company as being one of the many examples of micro-aggressions? I also wondered why she hadn't included falling asleep among them.

As you might have gathered, Rushdi's elucidation had failed to cast any meaningful light on the finer points of AI for me, but there then followed something which I thought I vaguely understood. This AI was, apparently, a bit like sophisticated computer software. In other words, a sophisticated computer programme. Aha! I mean, my desktop computer operates on Microsoft Windows, and that is computer software – this much I knew. So when, in the context of AI, we talked about a machine or a bot or a model, we meant software! My elation was, however, short-lived because Rushdi stressed that training AI was very different from normal software development. Oh dear! Is nothing in life simple any more? So what apparently happened was that engineers would amass the data and construct a rough blueprint of the AI model, but then the system in effect assembled *itself*, processing the training data and updating *its own* structure. Goodness me – the system assembled *itself and updated its own structure!* But what if it made mistakes? When Rushdi added that each training step tweaked the AI model in fundamentally unpredictable ways, I got seriously concerned. I mean – *unpredictable*, come on!

It appeared that I was right to be worried because Rushdi then proceeded to outline how things could go wrong. My ears definitely pricked up when he mentioned hallucinations. After all, Crystal had told me that AI could hallucinate, and what I understood was that this was when AI produced false information, creating nonsense, which, apparently, did happen. I defy you not to be worried. So I listened intently. Rushdi did indeed say that an AI model could make mistakes if it was trained on data reflecting human biases; if I'm not mistaken, he called this 'data distribution shifts'. He also explained that, because AI models generated responses based on statistical patterns learnt from large datasets rather than by actually *verifying* facts in those datasets, they could easily make up facts. As if this wasn't bad enough, Rushdi warned us that it was going to get harder to find a population of data that wasn't biased, so machines were going to learn unconscious biases. Were we *really* ready to unleash this AI onto the world?

But the gloomy scenario was about to get even gloomier: apparently, when you took AI-generated content and then kept feeding it back to AI over and over again, the systems would start making significant errors and producing nonsense. So *this* is how they hallucinated!

I was beginning to get extremely worried, but worse still was to come: Rushdi said that the degradation of model performance could lead to a complete model collapse. Blooming heck – a *complete model collapse!* By the time he had enlarged on two stages of model collapse, three types of model errors and computer-related perils which could be exacerbated by AI, such as pronounced algorithmic bias, unchecked online radicalisation, widespread cyber-attacks and ubiquitous surveillance, I was on the verge of panic. This sounded worse than a nuclear war!

Just as I started thinking that AI was about to wreak havoc all over the world and that we were all doomed, Rushdi assured us that humans were not about to become surplus to requirements. Phew! I will take humans any day – even if they are of the calibre of some of our senior managers. But I immediately thought about our poor teachers and wondered if Rushdi knew about what was in store for them. As you will now be aware, he was hardly ever in the office. Our poor teachers aside, I was reassured by his explanation that we needed humans in the loop because AI models were neither sentient nor entirely autonomous. Instead, they were elaborate pieces of software incapable of solving problems on their own. After being bombarded with all this hype about AI, one found it gratifying to learn that there was something it was *incapable* of! Hang on, hang on, can you get bombarded with hype? Yes, I think you can.

I'm delighted to report that Rushdi's peroration finished on a high note: he said that AI models relied on human beings to create and prompt them and then either to apply or to discard machine-generated results. My main takeaway was thus that, while AI might be revolutionary, it still depended on human judgement. I must say that this made me feel considerably better. On the other hand, if humans were so instrumental in the operation of this AI, how would we manage at FART? After all, none of us – apart from Rushdi, that is – was remotely capable of constructing an AI model.

As before, however, there was no time to ponder this unsettling question because Nota started thanking Rushdi profusely before imploring us to put our hands together. Needless to say, we all complied with great enthusiasm – particularly the ladies – although Aston, who had been roused by the riotous applause from his latest slumber (after my initial intervention, he had fallen asleep again), joined in with great vigour.

When the ovation finally died down – and it took quite a while – Nota announced to the audience: "Rushdi will now take your questions. I'm sure there is nothing he can't illuminate."

"*Explicate*," hissed Inco.

At this precise moment, colleagues started shifting in their seats uncomfortably and looking around as if they wanted to be the first to spot who the brave questioner might be. If Theo had been with us, he would doubtless have wanted to interrogate Rushdi in a most probing and incisive manner, but, unfortunately, he happened to be on annual leave. Although, indubitably, it wasn't unfortunate for *him:* the Bahamas sounded lovely at this time of the year. Actually, the Bahamas sounded lovely at *any* time of the year. The uncomfortable silence that followed Nota's invitation probably didn't last as long as it appeared, but the audience was nevertheless manifestly relieved when she rubbed her hands with visible satisfaction and delivered her killer wrap-up: "No questions? Excellent, excellent! This means that we have achieved absolute clarity – *absolute clarity*. A most successful elucidation."

"*Peroration*," hissed Inco.

"A most successful peroration. The lunch will be served in the lobby."

We all trooped out, with Aston advancing at a much faster pace than other colleagues. He came to an abrupt halt by a gleaming vessel with something steaming, which he was now ladling onto his plate. I'm sure I don't have to describe the sumptuous banquet laid on for us. If you want reminding, just visit my previous description. Again, Crystal, Viv, Stu and I made for the salads, and Stu regaled us with two jokes about AI.

"What is an AI bot's favourite music?"

"Pray, tell."

"Algorhythms, ho, ho, ho! And do you know that AI will never take away my job?"

"Why is that, Stu?"

"Because only an idiot would do my job, ho, ho, ho!"

Viv nodded. "Actually, you've got a point there, Stu. Maybe the bot's intelligence will save our poor pedagogues from extinction: who would be a teacher these days? Even if you are a machine."

"Look at Millie, look at Millie!" exclaimed Crystal suddenly.

We all turned around and could see Millie practically spoon-feeding Rushdi. The girl had it bad, no question about it. I'm sure you won't be surprised to learn that, in his arsenal, Stu had a joke which might appeal to her once she had recovered from her Rushdi affliction. Given, however, that she was currently in its throes, he shared it with us.

"A teacher asks little Johnny what he'd like to do when he grows up. 'I'd like to be a dustbin man,' replies little Johnny. 'Why is that?' asks the teacher. 'Because dustbin men have a good work-life balance,' says little Johnny. 'Why do you think that?' probes the teacher. 'Because they only work one day a week.' Ho, ho, ho!"

10

The Secret of Waterstones, Uncovering Dalliances and Undressing to Mate

On his return from Nassau, Theo reported that he had bumped into our Foremost Authoritarian and Bona there. Apparently, it was rather an intimate affair in one of the city's high-class restaurants. I wondered what Nota would have to say about this if she knew. Not to mention his wife. Anyway, Theo, *our* Theo, did cast further light on AI, but, before I can return to this – albeit only briefly, so please don't panic – I must report on the incredible progress I had made with Dew and Dali. Or, rather, on the progress they *themselves* had made. Having started from a lower base, Dali had had quite a bit further to go than Dew, and I was mightily impressed with the girl. In addition to my earlier language points, we covered pronouns, and Dali was now using demonstrative pronouns in phrases such as 'these/those things' rather than 'them things'. We also tackled verbs, so 'it were' became 'it was' and the verb 'joke' went back to being intransitive ('you're joking' rather than 'you are joking me'), with correct question tags having now practically replaced Dali's 'innit', although this usage did require a lot of practice. Regular and irregular verbs as well as irregular noun forms presented both girls with some challenges, which were, however, quickly overcome. And Dali's ubiquitous adjectives had started being replaced by adverbs in the contexts requiring the latter.

There were many more salient points of syntax we covered, but I'm mindful that not all that many people share my all-consuming passion for English grammar. Particularly if they are native speakers. Actually, some seem to think that English has no grammar at all. Then again, who can blame them? My finger points at Waterstones. Don't get me wrong, it's a fantastic bookseller, and I love it with a passion because it sells my books. But take this scenario: you go in and ask for books on English – where do they direct you to? To the reference section, of course. And their reference section is absolutely amazing, literally brimming with dictionaries and thesauruses – a vocabulist's paradise! But are there any books on English grammar there? Even though you scour the top shelves and look under the stairs, you cannot find any. So you start suspecting that English has no grammar – not unreasonably, if you ask me. Particularly if you were never taught English grammar at school – an astonishing state of affairs which persisted from the sixties to the late eighties.

But, of course, they have hundreds and *hundreds* of books on English grammar there: the secret is to delve into the section called English as a Foreign Language. As you can imagine, it has been my go-to destination ever since I settled in this wonderful country over four decades ago, which is why my house is filled to the rafters with English grammar books. But, unless they teach EFL, the lovely natives don't tend to stray there, so they return home thinking that English has no grammar. Anyway, that's my theory.

Returning to my tuition of Dali and Dew, in view of my allegedly 'speaking funny', I had outsourced pronunciation to Viv, who became my able teaching assistant. And I was careful to go easy on the slang expressions used by the girls: after all, vocabulary does evolve all the time, and we oldies have to accept that each generation creates its own colloquialisms and colourful expressions. I merely pointed out that, in more formal contexts such as employment, it was best to use them sparingly and left it at that. Grammar, however, was an entirely different kettle of fish, grammatical changes unfolding slowly over a long period of time. In any case, they were few and far between – if you take one's lifespan as the period under examination, that is.

I was delighted that both girls had started using my dictionary and thesaurus, the latter having convinced Dew that it wasn't a dinosaur. I was now permanently keeping both in the office, having plenty of others at home. Admittedly, we first needed to brush up on the alphabet – Dali, in particular, hadn't initially been able to tell her alpha from her gamma. But the alphabet having been mastered, I was stunned by an incident which was a direct result of Dali's newly acquired bibliographic competence. It was so unexpected that I feel compelled to enlarge on it here.

There weren't many of us in the office, for our cluster was having another action-packed day: Aston was attending a meeting of the Current Government Thinking Committee, Millie was attending a meeting of the Shared Vision Committee, Mala was attending a meeting of the Common Purpose Committee, Stu was attending a meeting of the Digital Technology Advisory Forum, Viv was attending a meeting of the Inter-Divisional Liaison Group and Dew was attending a meeting of the House, Lift and Stairwell Committee. It looked as though the other clusters occupying our floor were similarly engaged.

On entering the largely deserted office, Dali gave me a solemn look before saying, "You've changed your name, Ali, 'aven't… haven't you?"

"Well, not officially, but for here, yes."

"Gucci. And Theo, he has changed his name?"

"Yes, he has, he has."

"And I have also changed me… my name."

"You have *also* changed your name, Dali – really?"

"Defo: I'm now Delia."

"It's a lovely name, Dali… Delia, but why?"

What transpired was that, once Dali… I mean Delia had mastered the alphabet and learnt where, in the dictionary, to look for the words she wanted to check, she came across the noun 'dalliance'. Having uncovered its meaning, she immediately twigged what the provenance of Dali-Ance was. So she decided to take decisive action. And who can blame her? That's initiative for you. Naturally, I was most supportive.

"I'm sure everyone will love your new name, Da…

Delia. We'll tell them as soon as they come back from their meetings, won't we?"

"Defo; *I* will."

Of course, of course, it was her decision – not mine. As you can imagine, on their return my work colleagues immediately embraced Delia – both literally and figuratively – and the frenetic pace of our work continued. There then came the time to review what our cluster had thus far gathered by way of nourishment for our AI model, so several of us – including *our* Theo but excluding Rushdi – went to Edinburgh. On the thirtieth floor. The House, Lift and Stairwell Committee meeting which Dew had earlier attended must have produced a concrete result because the lift was enjoying a brief period of functionality. Strictly speaking, neither Dew nor Da... Delia needed to attend our gathering because they were very junior, but I had asked Aston to include them: it would be an excellent learning opportunity for them.

Reassuringly, Theo explained that we *ourselves* didn't have to worry about constructing our AI model, a task which would be carried out by Rushdi and a group of other computer whizzes he was assembling. Theo also said that our AI would be generative, which took us a bit by surprise because it was something Rushdi hadn't mentioned. Or maybe he had, but I found his peroration overwhelming at times and couldn't help occasionally tuning out. When we asked Theo what generative AI was, he explained that it was a subset of artificial intelligence used to produce texts, images, videos – stuff like that. Well, if we were going to do away with the entire teaching profession, we definitely needed our AI to produce texts, images and videos, so this was highly relevant to us.

We again heard that AI models relied heavily on the data they were trained on and that it was our job to identify high-quality training materials in quantities sufficient to represent what the model was trying to learn. Otherwise, it would be likely to spew out nonsense, and we would all be screwed. Then again, maybe this would save our unfortunate teachers from extinction. For a brief moment, I considered the possibility of sabotaging the whole operation – after all, I love teachers, having been one myself. But I soon came to my senses. Hubby and I might have to buy a bigger house to accommodate all my books on English grammar, so I needed the money.

In any case, we had already harvested tons of the stuff from across education in all four nations making up the United Kingdom and were, on that particular day in Edinburgh, about to commence its highly analytical review to make sure it would make suitable fare for our generative AI. We first turned our attention to materials pertaining to assessment: after all, checking their students' progress was an important part of each teacher's role. There was much I wanted to bring to my colleagues' attention, starting with one of the documents produced for the Scottish Curriculum for Excellence.

"Look at the enlightened policy our Scots comrades-in-arms had come up with."

Coursework assessment will be assessed by teachers.

"What do you think about this nonsense?"
"Why is it nonsense, Ali?"
"Because it says that *assessment* will be assessed, Dew.

But what they were trying to say was either that *coursework* would be assessed by teachers or that coursework assessment would be *conducted* by teachers. Or *carried out*."

"Cool beans."

"That's what I call circularity, Dew. This mistake is actually quite common: I've just heard on the radio that 'the power of the internet is very powerful'."

"Isn't it, Ali?"

"No, not *the power*. You can say either that the internet is very powerful or that the power of the internet is very considerable."

"Cool beans."

"Actually, I have also found quite a few examples of circularity in FART's bumf I've already looked at. Listen to this: 'Achievement of higher grades should not be achievable simply through the accumulation of more marks' – how can you achieve *achievement?*"

"So what would you say, Ali?"

"'*Higher grades* should not be achievable'. Or take this: 'Use of IT can be used to encourage a paperless environment' – how could you possibly *use* a use?"

"You mean… you mean *IT* can be used?" ventured Delia.

"Well done, Delia! Or 'Use of IT can be *made*'."

"Gucci."

Stu's chortle was accompanied by the usual twinkle in his eye. "But you still won't end up with a paperless environment."

"Maybe not, but at least you won't make yourself look silly. Or this: 'The Course develops understanding needed to understand contemporary business'."

Dew was quick with her correction: "Develops understanding of contemporary business?"

"Absolutely, Dew; you've both cracked it. But that's just a handful of examples; I have found many more similar ones in our documents. Doesn't the stuff get edited here?"

"It does – by our Editorial Department, ha, ha, ha!"

"In that case, they can't be particularly good, Crystal."

"*Particularly* good? I've told you: Ignor and Phillis haven't a bloody clue. Wait till they get their grubby paws on your writing!"

"What if my writing has no errors?"

"Don't you worry: by the time they have finished with it, it will have plenty, ha, ha, ha!" roared my fellow alien.

We then reviewed a document on positive marking. It explained that teachers should give students credit for what they get right but shouldn't deduct marks for anything their pupils might have got *less right*. It was supposed to be a very important principle, endorsed by the Committee for the Resounding Approval of Policies, Transformational-Policy Committee, the Cerebral Forum, the Overall Direction Steering Group and the Blue-Sky-Thinking Executive. The document further asserted that, without positive marking, students' self-esteem would be likely to suffer an irreparable damage, leading to all sorts of mental-health problems in future. It then gave an example taken from a student's examination paper, which went like this:

If you gess but you dont gess hia nuf you undress to mate.

The document proceeded to explain that positive marking should be applied to such work because, despite the highly creative spelling, the definition given by the student was nevertheless correct.

"Definition of *what?*" enquired Dew.

"It was supposed to be a definition of underestimating."

"How do you mean, Ali?"

"Apparently, what this student was trying to write was: 'If you guess, but you don't guess high enough, you underestimate.'"

While Crystal, Viv and Stu were busy laughing, I turned to Aston. "Surely, we can't feed this nonsense to our bot; if we do, these digital teachers will be talking gibberish, and we will all be sacked."

"And the poor bot will get indigestion, ho, ho, ho!" roared Stu.

My mentor having cogitated for a brief moment, it was agreed to add the document to the reject pile. Another manual decreed that all practical qualifications would have to include 'practical' in their title, citing *Practical Widget and Gadget Making* as an example. Naturally, I had to object to such usage, which I identified as tautology.

This was, however, immediately met with fierce resistance from Mala. "We do biology, geology and psychology, but we *definitely* don't do tautology, Ali. You'll get there – eventually."

I then had to explain that tautology was a fault of style where a word or statement was needlessly repeated to restate an idea in different words. The title given in the manual was thus tautological because widget and gadget *making* was practical by its very nature, which made the adjective 'practical' tautological. I quickly gave my colleagues further examples of tautology I had come across.

"'Acceptable performance in this unit will be the satisfactory achievement of the Summative Standards' – what's tautological there?"

Unsurprisingly, Crystal, Viv, Theo and Stu were ready with the answer, but I asked them to give both girls a chance.

"Hmm, perhaps 'satisfactory'?"

"Well done, Dew!"

Noticing a quizzical expression on Delia's face, I gave her a clue: "Have you ever heard of *unsatisfactory* achievement?"

"Hmm… not really."

"That's exactly why we must omit *satisfactory*. But this sentence is illogical anyway because performance itself is not the same as achievement."

"So… so what would you say, Ali?"

"'Acceptable performance in this unit will be confirmed by the achievement of the Summative Standards.' And how about this one: 'This will improve students' learning experience positively across the curriculum' – how would you correct this?"

"I would… I would… maybe remove 'positively'?" offered Dew.

"Absolutely: an improvement is always positive. And how about this one: 'This will provide a positive incentive for students to improve their literacy and numeracy'?"

"Oh, this is similar: an incentive is something positive."

"Spot on, Dew!"

"Unless it's perverse, ho, ho, ho!"

"Oh, shut up, Stu!"

Stu's clowning notwithstanding, I was in my element. "There is a lot of tautology about: *collaborate together, good benefit, mutual cooperation, new beginning, new innovation, past history, recall back, revert back, share the same, unite together, successfully give up, unsuccessfully fail, positively improve/support/enhance* – there are literally countless examples."

"But we are always saying *past history*," objected Mala.

"I bet you are, but history is always past – have you ever heard of *future* history?"

Dew was quick with a firm, "Never."

"Exactly, Dew. And I bet you are also saying *forward planning*."

"All the time."

"But planning is *always* forward, isn't it? When did you last plan *backwards?*"

"Hmm, never."

"My point exactly."

Our reject pile was growing alarmingly quickly, and other colleagues were also coming up with language horrors uncovered in the documents penned by some of the country's finest.

Opening one sitting on top of her own little pyramid, Crystal said: "Read this: 'Responses required in assessment would be best structured to require more than the minimum standard of the assessment standard.' This is supposed to be assessment guidance – can you imagine?"

"But what does this mean *exactly*, Crystal?" asked Dew.

"Probably that assessment tasks should be structured in a way enabling students to demonstrate a range of ability – or something along those lines."

"So... so why didn't they say so?" enquired Delia.

"I imagine they were simply not up to it."

"Proper mingin'."

"And listen to this: 'The level of learner support and the sophistication of responses expected would be a useful factor in ensuring progression rather than repetition' – what do you think they were trying to say?"

"Hmm..."

"Uhm..."

This gobbledygook having defeated both girls, Stu offered the following suggestion: "'As students progress, they should be offered less support and are expected to come up with more sophisticated responses' – something like that."

After Crystal and I congratulated Stu on his impressive powers of deduction, I shared another example of assessment guidance – this one produced by our very own organisation – making sure that they could all see it.

> *Schools' must ensure arrangements' for any coursework is controlled under rigorous conditions'.*

"What an awful muddle!" exclaimed Crystal.

"No, it isn't!" protested Mala, who, in her previous incarnation, was one of the authors of FART's guidance on coursework assessment.

"I'm afraid it is, Mala. What they should have written

is 'Schools must ensure that all coursework is carried out under rigorously controlled conditions'."

"But we know what we mean."

"That's not the point."

"What *is* the point?"

"To actually *say* what you mean. And, as you are saying it, not to fall into the proximity trap."

"Into *what*?"

"The proximity trap; there is the subject-verb disagreement there, Mala."

"No, no, no: there was no disagreement on any subject there."

"I mean in this sentence; arrangements *are* – not *is*."

"But coursework *is!*" interjected Aston in a tone which suggested that he felt quite sure-footed. "You'll get there, Ali – eventually."

"That's *exactly* why this error is called the proximity trap, Aston: writers often make the verb agree with the nearest noun rather than with the subject; the subject in the subordinate clause is the plural *arrangements* – not the singular *coursework*."

"The subject we are talking about here is that schools had better make damn sure they don't bring coursework into disrepute, right?"

"No, no, I mean *grammatical* subject."

"You and your grammar – change the record."

At this point, Stu regaled us with a joke about disagreement: "What do you call a disagreement between a vegan and a vegetarian?"

"What do you call it, Stu?"

"Beef."

I, however, wasn't quite finished with the coursework exemplar, which, I felt, couldn't possibly be fed to our bot. "But, Aston, these three greengrocers' apostrophes—"

"Leave greengrocers out of it, for Pete's sake."

"Don't you remember what I've said? That we don't need an apostrophe at the end of a regular plural. Unless it's about possession."

"Let me tell you something, Ali: schools would much rather someone else took possession of coursework."

"But this is not about schools!"

Stu leant back in his chair and laughed. "Too right, it isn't: after we have finished, there will be *no* schools."

Dew, her head slightly cocked, was twirling her ponytail , clearly pondering something.

"So is it DVDs – without the apostrophe – or DVD's – with the apostrophe? I often see DVD's written with the apostrophe – is that not right, Ali?"

"A great bit of deduction, Dew. We don't use the apostrophe with *any* regular plurals – including the plural forms of acronyms and abbreviations, such as DVDs, CDs, MPs, LEAs, PhDs or VDUs. Or with decades written as numbers, such as 1960s, 1970s, 1990s and so on."

"Cool beans; I'll remember that."

Further examples of gobbledygook came in thick and fast – some just about intelligible, others entirely impenetrable, the following falling into the latter category.

> *The development of peer evaluation skills' can be developed using strategies like encouraging students' in groups or individually to assess each others presentations in terms of how using*

> *PowerPoint, presentation skills, content and sources' used etc and two stars and wish when they peer mark work to ensure they are thinking about what made the work good but how it could have been improved.*

We continued in a similar vein, tossing our harvest onto the reject pile. Things didn't look good for our AI bot, and I was even beginning to feel sorry for it. Fed on a diet such as this, how was it ever going to usurp our esteemed educators? But maybe it was all a ploy on the part of the aforementioned educators? They might have got wind of what was in the offing and started producing gibberish on purpose. Now, there was a thought.

11

Homophones, Flippers, Fishmongers and Casualties

Having been warned of a particularly heavy day ahead, we had been ordered to report for duty earlier than usual. We were thus engrossed in our respective assignments when Aston's mighty frame appeared on the horizon. Forgetting all about our cluster huddle, he lowered himself into his chair, which responded with an alarming-sounding creak.

"How was the Marketing and Market Penetration Issues Focus Group, Aston?" enquired Mala with an energetic forward thrust.

"That was last night; we had a twilight session at the Grand Central Metropolitan, you know what I'm saying."

Dearie me: a *twilight* session? Little wonder Britain has the longest working hours in Europe.

"Basically, we seem to have penetrated the market rather successfully. Although there's still issues to resolve – there always is, right? The dinner wasn't bad either, you know what I'm saying. What we had *this morning* was the Overall Direction Steering Group."

"So how's the overall direction these days, Aston?" enquired Stu with what seemed to me suspiciously like feigned interest.

"Jolly good. Basically, we're getting lots of new steer. I'm gonna email you my notes – give me a sec."

Spotting a window in the proceedings, Stu quickly dived in with a direction joke. "As Bert and Joe are driving a tractor along a narrow country lane, a sports car is heading towards them extremely fast. Trying to avoid them, the car swerves, loses control, careers into a field and explodes. 'Good job we weren't in that field,' says Bert to Joe."

Ignoring the joke, Aston performed his usual stretch-pat routine and announced, "I've just emailed my notes to you."

The notes started with this sentence.

> *This is to conform that the Overall Direction Steering Group wants it's Key Policy Decision to be quoted in all reports, otherwise it will loose it's impact all staff are expected to comply.*

It took me a wee while to compose myself. "Look, Aston, I know that homophones are all over the place, but—"

"No, no, no: they are *not*, you know what I'm saying. We would *not* tolerate homophobes in our organisation, would we, Mala?"

"We *so* wouldn't! Ask Millie."

"No, no, I didn't mean homophobes – I was talking about *homophones*, Aston."

"What's that when it's at home?"

"Words which sound the same but are spelt differently, for example: *aloud/allowed, bear/bare, bread/bred, days/daze, dear/deer, ewe/yew, hair/hare, leak/leek, mail/male, main/mane place/plaice, roll/role* and *wine/whine*. Sometimes, there are more than two similarly sounding words, for example *pair/pare/pear* or *to/too/two*."

"What's this got to do with anything, for Pete's sake?"

"Well, *it's* with the apostrophe and *its* without the apostrophe are also homophones. You've written *it's* key policy decision and *it's* impact – with the apostrophe – but it should be *its* – with no apostrophe. Because it's about possession."

Aston smirked. "You'd better make up your mind: one minute, you reckon that the apostrophe is for possession and, the next, that it isn't."

"But, Aston, we *do* use the apostrophe to indicate possession with *nouns*, but *it* is a *pronoun* – it's different with pronouns. *It's* with the apostrophe signals an abbreviation, and *its* without the apostrophe possession."

"I have a homophone joke for you," interjected Ant. "Bert, who is bald, keeps tattooing rabbits on his scalp. 'Why do you keep doing that?' asks Matt. 'Because they say rabbits look like hairs,' replies Bert."

I wasn't quite done with Aston, though. "And the verb you want is spelt 'lose' – with only one 'O' – not 'loose', which is an adjective."

My mentor smirked. "Is it now?"

"Cross my heart and hope to die; you may have loose morals—"

"Careful, careful, Ali: I certainly do *not!* We don't tolerate insults here, you know what I'm saying."

"No, no, it was just an example of the adjective 'loose'. It's a classic misspelling, and—"

"Aston, may I have a word please. In private. And Mala." Engrossed in my linguistic exposition, I didn't notice Inco approach us. Our Enthusers and Directors had their own offices along the edges of our large open-plan space, and Inco had just emerged from his.

"Righteo, boss," said Aston with an energetic nod confirming his readiness to comply. Unfortunately, his chair refused to release his posterior, and the poor man – half bent, with the chair firmly clasped round his rear end – started wiggling furiously to extricate himself from his embarrassing predicament. The chair thrashed in the air but persisted in its refusal. Seeing his plight, Mala dashed over and grabbed an armrest. "Come on, Viv, grab the other one!" After a not inconsiderable amount of jerking and pulling, they managed to release Aston from his vexatious trap, and both men, accompanied by Mala, disappeared from view. It must have been all those working lunches, I thought.

"What did you mean by classic, Ali?" enquired Dew.

"I meant classic misspellings: confusing the verb *practise* with the noun *practice*, the verb *advise* with the noun *advice*, the verb *affect* with the noun *effect*, the verb *lose* with the adjective *loose*, *principal* with *principle*, *your* with *you're*, *there* with *their*, *complement* with *compliment*, *dependent* with *dependant*, *flare* with *flair*, *stationery* with *stationary*, *trailed* and *trialled*, *rational* with *rationale*, *moral* with *morale*, *emphasis* with *emphasise*, *confirm* with *conform* – there are so many. Some are homophones, of course; you've seen the confusion between *its* without the apostrophe and *it's* with the apostrophe."

The girl nodded.

"And have you noticed Aston's punctuation?"

"What's wrong with it?" asked Delia. It seemed that I didn't need the title of Enthuser to be able to enthuse: the girl appeared genuinely interested in my linguistic exegeses.

"Well, those run-on sentences for a start."

"What are run-on sentences?"

"Sentences not separated by any punctuation. Aston's email has at least two individual sentences, but he didn't use any punctuation before the last."

"Which is the last sentence?"

"'All staff are expected to comply'. You can't just tack this sentence onto the preceding one: you need either a full stop or a semi-colon."

"Not a comma?"

"No: that would be the comma splice."

"What's that?"

"It's also an error; he's used the comma splice before 'otherwise'."

"But what is it *exactly?*"

"The comma splice is a comma which is often wrongly used between closely related independent clauses instead of a semi-colon, a full stop or a connective. But run-on sentences are even worse. So what else could he have used before 'all staff'?

"Maybe… maybe another semi-colon?" ventured Dew.

"Possibly. But, if we used a semi-colon before 'otherwise', it would definitely be better to put a full stop there. And—"

I was then interrupted by Aston, who had returned with Mala, brandishing this command: "Inco wants us to go. Five minutes!"

I wondered if the firmness of his directive was supposed to compensate for his earlier embarrassing predicament.

"What size flippers do you take?" asked Mala, who seemed to be privy to something I was not. "We have small, medium and large."

"I don't know: I've never worn flippers."

"You so will today."

"Are we going diving? Will I need a wetsuit as well?"

"No, no, just flippers. What's your shoe size?"

"Five."

"So you'd better go for small then."

"Will do, Mala. But why do I have to wear flippers?"

"For our motivational and team-building event."

"Are we having a motivational and team-building event?"

"We so are!"

"But why didn't they tell us earlier?"

"Because nobody would have turned up, ho, ho, ho!" interjected Stu.

"But... but if it's to motivate us and that, surely..."

Crystal was now laughing as well. "You will soon find out why, ha, ha, ha!"

"But... but why do we need flippers, Mala?"

"To get in the mood."

Chivvied by Aston, our cluster beat the familiar path to the Grand Central Metropolitan alongside everyone else. In the lobby, we were greeted by Ira Scible, who worked further away on our floor. On the table next to him sat three piles of flippers: small, medium and large. Primed by Mala, I asked for a pair of small ones.

"Put them on now, please."

"*Now?*"

"That's what I've just said, isn't it?"

Blimey, he is rather irritable, I thought.

Although my flippers put up a spirited defence, I managed to gain the upper hand – though not without a struggle. The task accomplished, I followed Aston and Mala, who looked resplendent in their respective flippers. Suddenly, I heard the scream, "Holy mackerel!" I quickly turned round and saw Hudson River, an American working two floors above, prostrate on the smooth parquet, his beflippered feet pointing towards the ceiling. Immediately, a small group of his colleagues gathered around him and tried to help him to his feet.

"You haven't broken anything, have you, Hudson?" enquired Ina Morata with heart-warming solicitude.

"Ouch... I hope not, ouch, no, I don't... ouch... think so, but these flipping flippers, ouch..."

"Thank goodness; we'll help you – it's just round the corner."

Ina and her little group of Samaritans escorted the limping Hudson to the conference room. I wondered if, on this occasion, we were on the ground floor because of this particular prop; trying to negotiate stairs would undoubtedly be a far trickier proposition. Barring this one unfortunate incident, we all made it safely, if rather clumsily, to the new conference room, which was even larger than that used on previous occasions. Along one of the walls, there was a row of tables covered by navy-blue tablecloths and groaning under the weight of Danish pastries, croissants, jam-smothered pancakes, etc, etc, etc – you get the picture.

Inside the room, there were numerous round tables – one for each cluster – which were covered by what looked uncannily like fishing nets and on which sat all manner of marine paraphernalia, albeit of the toy variety. Among them were plastic fishes, shells, ships and anchors as well as fluffy pink-and-yellow octopuses, each sporting a captivating smile.

Once we were all seated, Inco stood on the podium, with Nota taking a seat next to him. I noticed that neither was wearing flippers. And, although all ladies were supposed to be betrousered for the occasion, Nota wasn't. Perks of power, I reflected.

"Morning, troops, and welcome to this tectonic, monumental and pivotal motivational and team-building event. As is traditional, customary and prevalent, we are going to start with a highly inspirational motivation task. You will be shown an amazingly motivational film, and, after the film, there will be a reflectional exercise to secure that you achieve clarity, lucidity and precision about how best to go forward with the lessons learnt for the benefit of FART. Without further ado…"

Inco gesticulated towards a colleague at the back of the room, who was in charge of a sizeable projector and who was apparently going to show us this amazingly motivational film. The film, entitled *The Fish*, was about a group of grumpy fishmongers who hated their lot. And who could blame them: they had to get up at the crack of dawn, brave all weathers – and, let's face it, the weather in this wonderful country doesn't always live up to expectations – and then stand there and sell fish all day every day to equally grumpy customers.

So they hated it and hated it and hated it, and then, suddenly, they had this brainwave: from now on, they were going to enjoy every single moment of their job. There remained one small obstacle, however: they didn't actually know how to go about enjoying every single moment of their job. Then, one of them had another brainwave and decided that they needed to do something highly entertaining. And what could be more entertaining than throwing fish at each other – and at customers as well? Bingo!

So, rather than handling the fishes in the usual boring manner, they started throwing them at one another to the accompaniment of great big belly laughs. Naturally, they also needed to cheer their customers up, so they would throw the purchased fish at them as well. It was so funny: there is this middle-aged lady in this very smart coat, and, suddenly, this wet fish is flying at her. So she has no choice but to catch it and clutch it to her very smart coat, which is now dripping wet and has this stain at the front. She looks round and sees that everyone is falling about laughing, so what can she do? Plus, they are all big strapping males, so she gives this weak smile – well, more of a grimace really – in what looks like a desperate attempt to blend in. Granted, you can't call it laughter, but it's certainly better than nothing.

"Jolly good!" howled Aston.

"Brill, I'm liking it!" Who, do you think, could have said it?

"It's a slay!" exclaimed Millie.

"Cool beans!" agreed Dew.

"Gucci," concurred Delia.

"Braw!" bellowed Jock.

That, essentially, was how it went on for the rest of the film: the fishmongers kept on throwing their fish and, in the process, grew to love their job and simply couldn't wait to get out of bed to embrace another day. And that was it. When the movie ended, I looked at Crystal, who looked at Viv, who looked at Stu, who looked at me. Other colleagues were, however, clapping enthusiastically, and I even saw Aston slap his thigh; I had never seen Aston slap his thigh before.

"That was jolly good, jolly good indeed, you know what I'm saying. Now, let's have a brainstorm about how we can best go forward with the lessons learnt to the benefit of FART."

"You are triggering me – we can't!" exclaimed Millie.

Taken aback, we all looked at her quizzically, and Aston enquired: "Are you saying we should let such a valuable exercise go to waste? We must have a brainstorm, you know what I'm saying."

"No, no, you can't say this!"

"Say *what?*"

"The 'B' word!"

"You mean *brainstorm?*"

"Of course: some people find it offensive."

"You mean some people find it offensive when you suggest they have a brain, ho, ho, ho!" roared Stu. "You may have a point there: you couldn't possibly accuse some of our big cheeses of being encumbered with this organ, ho, ho, ho!"

While Millie sat there looking indignant, Viv offered the conciliatory: "So what can we say instead, Millie?"

"A thought shower, of course. It's the *correct* term."

Aston appeared amenable. "OK then, let's have a thought shower. Go on, everybody, put your thinking caps on."

Thankfully, Millie didn't seem to object to his reference to thinking – although I didn't quite see how this function could be performed without recourse to the brain, but that's by the by.

"I could source some fish," offered Mala helpfully.

"Jolly good, jolly good!"

"But… but, Aston, do you think we are supposed to take the film quite so literally?" This challenge came from Viv.

"Viv is right," asserted Stu. "I don't think throwing fish around is going to benefit us one bit. For a start, just imagine how messy it would get."

Trying to suppress a chuckle, Crystal nodded. "Yep, I am sure the lesson is far more subtle than that."

"Hmm, you might have a point there," reflected Aston. "What if you don't catch the fish in time, and it lands on top of all the *Missions, Visions, Principals, Policies, Pledges, Priorities, Initiatives and Strategies?*"

"So what could we throw instead?" pondered Mala.

"I know: *Digital Training Blueprints, Paradigms, Schemes and Strategies!*" exclaimed Millie.

"Brill; I'm liking it."

"No, no, no: far too heavy," countered Aston, "you might do someone a serious injury, you know what I'm saying. Can you imagine the implications for FART? Basically, the government grant..." The prospect of jeopardising our government grant was clearly so perturbing that it rendered him momentarily speechless.

"The Cerebral Forum's minutes then? Last year's look just about the right size," mused Mala.

"Hmm, that's certainly a possibility," conceded Aston. "I was also thinking about the Governmental Growth and Productivity Agenda."

"But surely, the message is *far more general* than that," dissented Crystal.

Aston furrowed his brow and twirled the end of his moustache. "Hmm, you mean that it's good to laugh? You may be right there."

It was now my turn to contribute to our reflectional debate. "Actually, our Well-Beings did write that it was good to laugh; in their latest bulletin."

"But what could we laugh about?" puzzled Mala.

"The number of our committees?" This tongue-in-cheek suggestion came from Stu.

Crystal was now openly laughing. "I'd say the linguistic ineptitude of Ignor, Phillis and the rest of our editorial team."

"No, seriously, it must be something to do with a positive attitude to work," said Viv.

"*A positive attitude to work?* Well, as long as we have our government grant..." cogitated Aston.

Stu chortled in his usual manner. "And a steady supply of amazingly motivational films, ho, ho, ho!"

It was then that Nota stood up, straightened her skirt, flicked her hair and said, "It's good to see you guys so highly motivated. Sorry to interrupt such a robust debate, but we need to move on: the next part of the event will be starting shortly. There will be a plenary before the close of play, so you will have the opportunity to engage in peer interface and cross-fertilisation. Please proceed to the lobby; there are some refreshments there; we need to rearrange the room. And you may now take your flippers off."

More refreshments – blimey, I thought, eyeing up the mountain of uneaten food in the conference room as I tore the flippers off my feet.

***

In the lobby, we found brand-new refreshments, with scones, chocolate cake, carrot cake, lemon cake and flapjacks taking pride of place on the side tables, which were covered by red tablecloths. It appeared that, like me, neither Crystal nor Viv could as much as look at a flapjack crumb, and both ladies joined me in the corner by the window. Soon, we were approached by Stu, who was looking particularly highly motivated.

"Apropos fishmongers hating their job, I have a hate joke for you. Carmel asks Mary, 'What's your pet hate?' Mary replies: 'When I forget his dinner', ho, ho, ho!"

***

"Welcome to the main team-building event," said Nota with a hair flick, "and let's extend a particularly warm welcome to our EEC colleagues, who will be hosting the event."

Raising both arms as if to celebrate mass, Nota turned to the three sharp-suited gentlemen forming a small but highly executive cluster in one of the corners. The conference room had now been cleared of all its tables and chairs and looked even more spacious than before. On the floor along one of the walls lay coils of rope, bits of sticks, pieces of strange-looking tubes and other curious implements looking rather out of place in a five-star hotel.

"Wow, I didn't think the EEC would want to bother with our team-building events," I whispered to Viv. "Don't they have the European economy to worry about?"

"This EEC stands for Events for Educational Corporations. They always run our team-building events."

One of the EEC gentlemen stepped forward, acknowledged Nota's introduction with a Japanese-style bow, wrung his hands and looked at us with a self-assured smile. "Thank you all for having us back again; it's always a pleasure and a privilege – *a pleasure and a privilege*." The other two EEC gentlemen nodded in earnest agreement.

"I bet it is – at several grand a pop," sniggered Stu.

"The first challenge will test your collaboration skills." The three EEC gentlemen divided our clusters into six teams, told each team to form a chain by getting each of us to hold hands with the colleague immediately ahead and the colleague immediately behind and then deftly lassoed each chain with a piece of rope. The rope was then tangled around us, and we were told to untangle it and free ourselves without using our hands, which were to remain firmly linked with those of our neighbours. This meant that we had to perform all sorts of unnatural contortions to try to free ourselves, and I finally understood why all ladies were supposed to wear trousers. The exercise did indeed demand twists and bends I had hitherto thought my body incapable of, the teams convulsing as if they were in death throes.

"My hair, my hair!" screamed Dew, whose ponytail had got caught in the rope, the mishap trapping her head and pulling it towards the floor. It took a great deal of team effort to rescue the poor girl, by which time Mala's team had somehow managed to untangle itself.

"Brill, we have finished, we have finished!" yelled Mala as she and her victorious comrades stood eagerly to attention.

I looked at her: her ravine had all but disappeared, her eyes were glistening, and her body, trembling with hopeful anticipation, made her resemble a whimpering puppy impatiently awaiting a treat. To everybody's surprise, the EEC gentlemen failed to acknowledge her triumphant salvo and continued circling round the five jerking, jolting, twitching, thrashing and writhing teams. Eventually, even ours had managed to free itself, although we came a miserable last – albeit with only minor injuries.

It was only then that one of the EEC gentlemen turned towards Mala. "Why didn't you try to help the other teams after you'd finished?"

"Uh? Rewind."

Another EEC gentleman concurred, "They did need succour."

"You'd need to be," sneered Mala.

"Sorry, I'm not sure I'm with you; you'd need to be *what*?"

"A sucker. No offence, but you'd need to be a sucker to help a competing team."

"No, no, I meant *succour* – help. We didn't say this was

a competitive challenge; it was all about cooperation. Both within and between teams. So why didn't you try to help the others?"

Mala, her mouth half-open, looked totally crestfallen.

"She is extremely competitive, and these events only make it worse," explained Viv after we both stopped giggling. I looked at Mala again, and there could be no mistaking the expression on her face: pure and unadulterated hatred. Blimey, I thought: if this is about team building, I am the Queen of Sheba.

After the tangled-rope challenge, there was an open-tin challenge, which, additionally, was to decide the fate of our planet. This open tin full of gooey stuff was sitting on the floor, and we were supposed to empty it in the air without touching it with our hands – or with any other part of our anatomy, for that matter. Since the success of this manoeuvre was supposed to save the world from an immediate extinction, the pressure was certainly on. That's where the ropes, sticks, tubes and the other implements came in: because we couldn't touch the tin, they were the things on which hinged mankind's fate.

The exercise certainly demanded much crawling and twisting on the floor, and, again, our trousers proved invaluable in protecting our dignity. Additionally, whoever found himself or herself outside the white circle drawn on the floor around, but some distance from, the tin would face an instant annihilation. After enduring a not inconsiderable amount of pushing, shoving and kicking, I decided that there were things worse than death and stepped outside the circle, whereupon I was quickly pronounced expired. I was thus able to observe the mayhem unfolding inside the circle with some detachment.

Mala, lying on the floor and supporting herself on both elbows, was making hoops with a piece of rope while shouting to Stu, "No, no, no, put this stick away, we so must get this rope round the tin – I'm making some hoops!"

"No way," screamed Ira, "we have to attach this piece of rope to this tube first – this tube is the right length! Bloody women!"

"Put that down, put that down: we don't need your tube – this stick will be much better," shouted Ina, waving a bit of stick in the air and, accidentally, poking Su in the eye. By the way, Su Pine was the PA to our elusive Foremost Authoritarian.

"Bloody women!" repeated Ira.

"Ouuuu!" howled Su, covering her face with both hands.

"Get the first aiders!" barked Al Manac, who was the first to rush to Su's side. She was swiftly surrounded by helpful colleagues and escorted out of the room, intervention which allowed the proceedings to continue.

"It's got to go in there – in there, in there! No, no – *in there!*" yelled Ignor.

"It won't go in; better tie it to this tube. Holy mackerel, not like this – like *this!*" hollered Hudson, now, clearly, fully recovered.

"Bolt ya rocket!" shouted Jock.

"Hold on, hold on, these pieces of rope are too long; we gotta shorten them first to get enough tension!" bellowed Aston.

From where I was standing, there was more than enough tension in the room already, but I had no say in the matter. I was soon joined by Crystal, who'd also breached the boundary between life and death. I could swear that I'd seen Mala elbow her unceremoniously into the death zone. The fun and games went on for some time until, finally, the tin was emptied in the air and mankind was saved. But since it wasn't Mala's idea that proved the clincher, it was apparent that her resentment only grew.

Other, more cerebral, challenges included the assassin, with Jock as the assassin, whom we managed to identify in the nick of time, and the fugitive, impersonated by Stu, who managed to evade capture and to reach sanctuary, causing Mala even greater frustration in the process.

Then we had another physically taxing challenge, which involved much jumping, hopping, lunging, pouncing and leaping to detach a rectangular object suspended from the ceiling. This was rather unfair, I thought, for it clearly favoured taller colleagues, although we were allowed to use props.

"I got it, I got it!" screamed Mala – somewhat prematurely, it transpired, for the suspended object, while indeed performing a swaying motion, remained attached to the ceiling nevertheless.

Suddenly, everything went pitch black…

***

I came to in a strange bed. There were tubes coming out of my nose, and the smell was… green. That's the only way I can describe it.

"She's coming round," said a voice somewhere. I turned in the direction of the voice and saw a figure dressed in white. The figure approached my bed and bent over. "Are you hurting?" it asked.

"Uhm... I'm not sure... where am I?"

"Accident and emergency."

"*Accident and emergency?* What happened?"

"We've been told that a colleague landed right on top of you. You were involved in some sort of jumping activity. In a five-star hotel."

"Who was it?"

"We don't know, but it was a female. You were lucky: with a male colleague, it might have been much worse. Can you move your head for me? Gently, gently!"

I slowly turned my head left and then right.

"Excellent. The X-ray shows a slight concussion, but we can't see any brain damage. We are going to keep you in overnight – just to be on the safe side."

"Oh no!"

"Don't worry, it's a standard precaution."

"No, no, you don't understand: I will have missed the plenary! And my very first meeting of the Committee for the Operational Reviews of Processes, Strategies and Endorsements!"

12

Ferrets, Apes and Mongooses

It had been a hectic time since our ill-fated team-building event, with all of us trying to forget the physical and mental scars left by the aforementioned and beavering away on our priority deliverables. Well, Mala still seemed to be reeling from her humiliations, but the rest of us had got over the experience. By the way, it was she who had landed right on top of me. I did forgive her, even though she hadn't even bothered to apologise. Anyway, on with the story. As soon as I entered the office on that particular day, I could sense an unusual undercurrent: the office atmosphere was definitely different. Did I detect a frisson of excitement in the air? Throughout the entire floor, colleagues, clustered in little groups, foreheads touching, were discussing something animatedly, with a few additionally waving their arms about.

Inco – *our* Inco – and Nota were standing in the middle of the floor debating something with great animation. Seeing them conduct their corporate affairs in full view of everybody was most unusual, for it had, by now, become clear to me that they preferred more refined, not to mention salubrious, surroundings. Even Inco Municado, who is usually either safely sealed off in his office or away on FART business and is seen at large only in meetings, darted across the office at an Olympic-standard speed.

I'm sorry that, having undoubtedly aroused your curiosity, I must now leave you hanging for a little while. This is because I'm duty-bound to report on a very important development concerning my star pupil, Delia. Not only was she now sharing a privately rented flat with Dew and Chardonnay, but she had orchestrated something truly remarkable. It was clear that the girl was enjoying working with us and that she appreciated earning her own money. She did actually say to me once that she valued the freedom of being able to choose the flat to rent rather than having to accept what she was given by the council.

So do you know what she did? She worked on her siblings and managed to convince each that getting a job would be a good idea. And they did! Obviously, theirs were entry-level positions, but, if they were as bright as her, they would undoubtedly progress. There was only one intransigent half-brother, who, apparently, persisted in his deeply held conviction that work was for bozos. It would appear that Terminator's, apparently congenital, allergy to earning one's crust rubbed off on the unfortunate boy, who was in danger of heading for the scrap heap before he even got a proper shot at life – what a waste!

And one of her younger half-sisters, Kaydelle, actually started working in our cluster, Delia having vouched for her with great vehemence. She proved to be a touchingly protective big sister, who tried to help Kaydelle, whom we were to call Delle, as much as possible. But, that morning, Delia was busy with Aston, so the youngster was tackling the task she had been entrusted with single-handedly. She approached me with a visible hesitation, so I smiled at her as warmly and encouragingly as I could.

"It's lovely to have you with us, Delle. I hope you will enjoy working with us."

"Fanks. Uhm… do you para… para…?"

"Paraphrase, Delle?"

"No, no, para… para…"

"Parachute?"

"A bit like parachute, like – in the air."

"You mean paraglide?"

"Totes; that's the one!"

"No, of course I don't paraglide. Why do you ask?"

"'Cos I 'ave to. So you don't 'ave them para… them fynks…?"

"If you mean a paragliding harness, no, I don't – should I?"

"No, no, no bovver, like. How 'bout 'orses?"

"What about horses?"

"Do you, like, ride an 'orse?"

"No, Delle, I can't ride a horse – should I?"

"No bovver, no bovver. So you don't 'ave no odd pairs, like?"

"*Odd pairs?* Well, I do have some odd socks, Delle, but they are not in pairs. They always get separated in the wash – drives me mad."

Before the youngster had the chance to protest, Crystal came to her rescue: "I think she means jodhpurs, Ali."

"Oh, I see. No, Delle, I don't have jodhpurs. But I could get some; I know a shop where they sell all sorts of riding paraphernalia."

"No, no, don't buy nuffink, like! How 'bout bungee-jumping?"

"What about bungee-jumping?"

"Do you do them jumps, like?"

"Not if I can help it, Delle, no. Anyway, after our team-building event I'm done with jumping. I got a concussion, you know. I was gutted, completely gutted: they had kept me in overnight, and I missed the plenary at the end. And my very first meeting of our CORPSE – can you imagine!" Seeing the quizzical expression on the youngster's face, I quickly added: "I mean the Committee for the Operational Reviews of Processes, Strategies and Endorsements."

The young girl gave me a look full of sympathy and resumed her interrogation: "And this ferret fyngy?"

"What ferret thingy, Delle?"

"I up, like."

"*I beg your pardon?*"

Attempting to stifle her chuckle so as not to upset the girl, Crystal was quick with her clarification. "She means 'high up'!"

"Of course, of course; sorry. But ferrets don't go high up – they do all their ferreting on the ground."

"Oh, Ali, she means via ferrata!"

"Sorry, sorry, Delle. If you mean whether I've been up a via ferrata, no, I haven't. I suffer from vertigo."

"Wicked! So you don't 'ave no 'elmit."

"A helmet? No, I don't. But, look, what's all this about?"

"How do you mean what's all this about, Ali? Haven't you heard? We so have a crisis – a serious crisis!" exclaimed Mala, who had suddenly materialised next to me.

"Oh dear, how awful, Mala! What sort of crisis?"

"A financial crisis."

"A *financial* crisis? Have they pulled our government grant, by any chance?"

"Oh count rare."

"Are you saying that some count is involved, Mala? In what way?"

Crystal, though, seemed to know that no aristocracy had had a hand in our financial crisis. "She means *au contraire*."

"That's *exactly* what I've said. You'll get there, Ali – eventually. Look—"

She was interrupted by Aston, still some distance away, who was exclaiming: "CC, CC!"

I thought it was an excellent suggestion: "A good idea, cost-cutting should help us."

But why were Crystal and Stu convulsed with laughter? Didn't they care about our financial viability?

"Why are you laughing? I, personally, think it's absolutely awful that we have a financial crisis."

"We… we always have a financial crisis, ho, ho, ho!"

"What do you mean *always*, Stu?"

"Always… always at this… ho, ho, ho… at this time of year, ho, ho, ho!"

"I'm not with you. If it's a recurring problem, couldn't we have done something to pre-empt it?"

"Not before March, no," chuckled Crystal.

I was now getting slightly annoyed. "Look, you are talking in riddles – both of you. I can't see what's so funny."

"You'll see in a minute. We can't spoil this for you – we just can't."

Since they, clearly, had an unfair advantage over me, there was nothing else to be said at that juncture.

"CC, CC!" echoed Mala. "Come on!"

It was then explained to me that CC stood for Cluster Circle: we were supposed to get our chairs in a circle for a quick conference, all our meeting rooms having already been taken. We all arranged ourselves in the stipulated formation, Aston's physiognomy having settled into an expression befitting a serious crisis. My curiosity was growing by the second.

"Basically, each cluster gotta suggest its preferred solution to this year's financial crisis, so we need to have a brain… uhm… a thought shower, right? Let's all… just a sec, where's the biscuits?"

"In your in-tray, Aston," helpfully pointed out Mala.

"Fetch them here, will you?"

With the plate of biscuits strategically positioned on the floor in the middle of our little circle, Aston turned on the thought shower. "Basically, I reckon we should go for ape this year, although I welcome other ideas, you know what I'm saying."

"You mean *go ape*, Aston? That would be fun."

"No, no, no, Ali: I suggest we go *for* ape."

"You mean to the zoo? Or were you thinking of going to Africa on some sort of fundraiser to avert our crisis? On the ape trail or something like that?"

"No, no, no: I mean the Adrenaline Package for Executives."

"O-o-o-o, I see: *APE*; of course, silly me. But what do you need this package for?"

"For our CBA, you know what I'm saying."

"You mean Cost-Benefit Analysis, Aston? What an excellent idea – just what an organisation needs in the time of crisis."

"Try Can't Be Arsed," chortled Stu.

Having impaled him on his killer stare, Aston proceeded with his explanation. "I mean our *Corporate Bonding Awayday*, Ali. In the past, we tried the Pamper Package, the Sports Package, the Arts and Crafts Package, the Adventure Package, the Self-Improvement Package, the Surprise Package, the Olympian Package, the Culture Package, the Bonding Package, the Skyline Package, the Fun Package and the Scenic Package, but me and Mala thought that, for this year, we should have a bash at this Adrenaline Package for Executives. Mala has done some preliminary research. What did you find out, Mala?"

"They do paragliding, horse riding, bungee-jumping, climbing, abseiling, gill scrambling, mountain biking, rafting, quad bike trails, aerial trekking, scuba diving, jet skiing and fly fishing."

"Ouky-douky, that's a jolly good offer, right?" asserted Aston, looking over his small but perfectly formed fiefdom with an undeniably self-satisfied expression on his face.

"Aye, aye."

"Awesome, I'm liking it."

"Cool beans."

"Sick."

"Gucci."

"Oh, and via ferrata, Aston – they also do via ferrata."

"Jolly good, Mala. What do *you* think, Stu? You are being rather quiet."

"To be honest, Aston, it doesn't bother me."

"How do you mean *it doesn't bother you?* It *should* bother you – we have to make the right decision: there's very little time before the end of the financial year, you know what I'm saying."

"Do we have to avert the crisis before the end of *this* financial year, Aston?"

"We do indeed, Ali, we do indeed."

"Oh dear, there's hardly any time left!"

"My point exactly. And what do *you* reckon, Crystal?"

"I'm afraid I'm with Stu on this one, Aston: in the end, it doesn't really matter which one we choose."

"How do you mean *it doesn't matter?* Of course it matters! For a start, there is the venue, and the costs vary widely. Some venues are *way* too cheap, you know what I'm saying."

"'Course they are, 'course they are," concurred Mala enthusiastically.

"Thank you, Mala. Then you have the corporate bonding activities – basically, the more activities, the higher the cost, right?"

"Aye, aye."

"Thank you, Jock. And then, there is the question of who supplies the gear for all the corporate bonding activities. Obviously, it would be preferable for us to buy all of it ourselves, you know what I'm saying. That's why I've asked Delle to do an equipment survey. Delle, you have all the details, don't you?"

The shy youngster nodded and passed the findings to Aston. Delia, who was sitting next to her, asked anxiously: "How did she do?" We all reassured her that her little sister had done just fine, but I thought to myself that I might be acquiring another tutee. Well, if she is as keen and sharp as Delia, it will be a pleasure.

Aston looked at the survey results and smiled broadly. "Jolly good, jolly good: it looks like we will have to buy virtually all the equipment for the APE activities—"

"*As if*, Aston." I know I shouldn't have interrupted him, but I've told you that I'm passionate about the English language, haven't I?

Aston gave me a hostile glare. "Don't contradict me, Ali! I know what I'm talking about, right?"

"Of course you do, of course you do, Aston, but we'd say: 'it looks *as if* we'll have to buy something' – not 'it looks *like*' – because 'like' isn't a conjunction. Not in formal English, anyway."

"So what do you reckon it is?" There was no mistaking the sarcasm in Aston's voice.

"Well, it can be a preposition…"

"My point exactly: my proposition is to buy all the gear, right?"

"No, no, not a proposition – *a preposition*. The Oxford English Dictionary – the twenty-volume one – says that using 'like' as a conjunction 'is now generally condemned as vulgar or slovenly'."

"We don't tolerate insults here, Ali, you know what I'm saying."

"But, Aston, it's a quote – *from The Oxford English Dictionary!*"

At this point, Crystal gave me a sharp kick in the shin and whispered: "Leave it, leave it."

Having glowered at me for a period which he must have judged to be commensurate with the gravity of my offence, Aston continued. "So it looks *like* we'll manage to spend quite a bit of dosh, you know what I'm saying."

Despite my chastisement, I couldn't contain my bafflement any longer. "*Spend*, Aston?"

"Indeed, indeed."

"But why should we be *spending* money?"

"Because we have a crisis – basically."

"So shouldn't we be *saving* money instead?"

"No, no, no, whatever gave you this idea?"

"Because that's what you do when you have a financial crisis. It's a basic rule of budgeting."

"No, no, no, we have to *spend* money, Ali. And lots of it, right?"

"So how exactly is it a crisis, Aston?"

"Basically, if we don't spend all the dosh we had been allocated for this financial year, they gonna cut our government grant next year, you know what I'm saying. And we don't have all that much time left. So we gotta move fast, right?"

"O-o-o-o, I see. But, if we haven't spent all of our grant, we obviously don't need what is left."

"We need every single penny, Ali."

"'Course we do, 'course we do."

"Aye, aye."

"But this is obviously a surplus. I'm sure the government could spend it on some worthy projects."

"Such as?"

"I don't know; give it to the nurses or the police – or maybe to the teachers – while they still exist. But we won't be abolishing them any time soon, surely. Not with all the rubbish that our AI bot is in danger of ingesting."

"Look, Ali, teachers have enough already; they don't need any more. SMUT's only gonna jack up their membership fees. You want to see their offices – so plush they could give the Grand Central Metropolitan a run for its money, you know what I'm saying."

"So perhaps we could finally beef up our defence spending. I mean, 2.3% is pitiful, and even 2.5% is not enough. Not with Trump sucking up to Putin and ready to throw Europe under a bus."

"No, no, no, we definitely need all the dosh we can get; even the Navigating Assembly and the Overall Direction Steering Group are agreed on this one. And they don't often see eye to eye, you know what I'm saying. We might not necessarily need the surplus *this* year, but who knows what's gonna happen in future? What if we have a change of minister? They might want us to scrap what we are doing and start on something entirely different. That doesn't come cheap, you know what I'm saying."

"It so doesn't, it so doesn't," concurred Mala with an energetic nod.

"Basically, they can turn policy on a sixpence, right? That's why we gotta get rid of all the surplus this financial year, Ali – better safe than sorry."

"I s-e-e-e, Aston; that's very… very prescient."

Stu gave me a wink and chortled. "That's one way of putting it."

"Thank you, Ali," said Aston, ignoring Stu and performing his familiar stretch-pat routine to the audible discomfiture of his chair. "Basically, this Adrenaline Package for Executives, it's a win-win, right? Now, I want you all to list any special requirements you might have; give me a sec."

We returned to our workstations and, soon, received from Aston an email entitled *Currant Financial Crisis*, which contained a two-column grid. The top of the left-hand column said *Mens Special Requirements*, and the top of the right-hand column said *Womens Special Requirements*.

"Terribly sorry, Aston, but this is about possession."

"No, no, Ali, this is about special requirements."

"What I mean, Aston, is that you need two apostrophes there. With *men's* and *women's*."

"Do I now?" There was the familiar sarcasm in my mentor's voice.

"Cross my heart and hope to die."

"But, in my supermarket, they don't use the apostrophe in *Mens Toiletries*."

"They wouldn't, would they, Aston? At the end of the day, it's a supermarket, so what do you expect? They are not exactly an authority on English, are they? You go there for granola – not grammar."

"A-a-a-a, but our Well-Beings never use the apostrophe in *Mens, Womens and Childrens Health*, so there!"

"You mean those same Well-Beings by whom we have been reliably informed that harbingers of doom are *profits*?"

Aston gave me a probing look, pondered my riposte for a moment and said, "Give me a sec." Very shortly, his amendment pinged into our inboxes. The grid now said *Mens' Special Requirements* and *Womens' Special Requirements*.

"But, Aston, these are irregular plurals."

"Listen, Ali, there's nothing irregular about our English. You'll get there – eventually."

"No, no, I'm talking specifically about irregular *plurals*. It's a grammatical term."

"Change the record, for Pete's sake."

"No, Aston, honestly, some English nouns form irregular plurals."

"Such as?"

"*Calf, deer, goose, half, knife, man, mouse, shelf, thief, tooth, woman.* They are called irregular because they don't form plurals in the usual way. So 'a man' will have an irregular plural because you can't say 'two mans'."

"Of course you can't say 'two mans' – do you think I'm stupid?"

"No, no, perish the thought, Aston – not with all your qualifications! I'm just giving you an example of a noun with an irregular plural."

"Your point being?"

"That you need the apostrophe *before* 'S' – *not* after."

"You reckon?"

"Cross my heart and hope to die; look." I quickly amended Aston's grid to read *Men's Special Requirements* and *Women's Special Requirements* and clicked on send.

"Talking about regular, I have a regular task for you," announced Mala, who had been tapping away determinedly. "I'm typing up our APE proposal for the Foremost Authoritarian and need to include one key selection criteria. What do you think is the most important criteria?"

"Ion, Mala."

"Who is Ian?"

"No, not Ian – ion: criter*ion*. Criter*ia* is plural, criter*ion* is singular."

"Is it? But I've never heard criter*on* – ever."

"Look, people use the plural *criteria* instead of the singular *criterion* all the time. But 'criteria' is an irregular plural; it's also a foreign plural."

"What do you mean by a foreign plural?" enquired Dew.

"Foreign plurals are plural forms of nouns of foreign origin."

"We have nouns of foreign origin, Ali?"

"Every other bloody thing is of foreign origin here," barked Ira Scible, who happened to be passing by en route to his desk in the corner. "That's why the country has gone to the bloody dogs."

As you will undoubtedly have guessed – I'm most impressed by your powers of deduction, by the way – Ira was well known for his irascibility, so we ignored his remark.

"Yes, English does have nouns of foreign origin, Dew."

Delia, who had been listening intently, joined in our confabulation: "Could you give us some examples, Ali?"

"*Criterion* – obviously, but also *analysis, stimulus, index, curriculum, phenomenon*, nouns like that."

"'Course she is meaning phenomen*um*, Delia."

"No, no, Mala, I do mean phenomen*on*."

"But we always say phenomen*um* – like curriculum – don't we, Aston?"

"We do indeed, we do indeed."

"But it's phenomen*on*, cross my heart and hope to die. And the plural is phenomen*a* – it's another example of a foreign plural."

"Foreign here, foreign there, foreign bloody everywhere." And with this parting remark, Ira was gone.

***

"I'm really worried," I unburdened myself to Stu in the kitchenette. In fact, I was so alarmed that I'd had to resort to fairly vigorous bouncing on one of our space hoppers to release some of the tension.

"Why?"

"This Adrenaline Package for Executives – all those corporate bonding activities…"

"Relax, Ali; you'll be fine."

"But it sounds much worse than the team-building event."

"Does it? I quite liked the sound of it, actually. In the past, we had some boring packages. The bonding and arts and crafts ones in particular. But this one might be fun."

"That's exactly what worries me, Stu. I don't think I could face any of those activities. Particularly after my concussion."

"So don't go."

"But would I get away with it?"

"To be sure, to be sure. Once you are booked, we'll still have to pay, and that's all that matters. As long as we get rid of the moolah, our big cheeses will be happy. Just call Aston at the last minute and make up some excuse – tell him it's bird flu or something like that."

"Can people get bird flu?"

"No idea, but Aston won't know either. He isn't the brightest light in the harbour, is he? Talking of which, I have a joke for you. Your man enters a police station, looks around, sees all the photographs on the walls and asks the desk sergeant, 'Who are all those pictures of?' The duty officer replies, 'Oh, they are just the people we are trying to catch.' The man looks surprised. 'Couldn't you catch them when you were taking these photographs?'"

"Oh, Stu, ha, ha, ha!"

"Glad you liked it, Ali. Here is another one – right up your street: it's about nouns of foreign origin. Your man, who is opening a new zoo, writes to the owners of a well-established one:

"Dear Sirs,
"I am opening a zoo and would be grateful for your assistance. Please send me two mongooses. A cheque is enclosed.

"Yours faithfully,
"Bear Brown

"He reads the letter back, pauses over 'mongooses', has a little think and says to himself, 'No, that doesn't look right.' He then crosses off 'mongooses' and, in its place, writes 'mongeese'. He looks at 'mongeese', has another little think and says to himself, 'No, that doesn't look right either.' He then crosses off 'mongeese' and, in its place, writes 'mongi'. He looks at 'mongi', has yet another little think and says to himself, 'No, that can't be right either. To hell with it!' He then crosses off 'mongi', writes 'Please send me a mongoose' and adds a PS which says, 'While you are at it, please send me another one.'"

13

Corporate Mayhem, Bombshells, Banquets and Jubilations

"I'm booking a taxi for Aston and Millie; anybody want to join them?" enquired Mala.

"But the Grand Central Metropolitan is just round the corner – why do we need a taxi?"

"We are not at the Grand Central Metropolitan today, Ali."

"We are not? So where are we?"

"Hilton."

"How come?"

"Because the Grand Central Metropolitan is fully booked."

"How come?"

Stu was quick with his theory, but was he being serious? "Everyone else must also be rolling out their new corporate identity today."

"Girls, do you want to go with Aston and Millie?"

"Thanks, Mala, we'll walk – it's not all that far," said Crystal.

"I'll go with them then. To be honest with you, the invalids will so need somebody to help them." Aston and Millie did indeed present a pitiful sight, the former trying to balance himself on reinforced crutches with what was clearly a considerable effort, his lower leg encased in plaster, the latter being swathed in bandages from top to toe, with only her eyes, nose, mouth and fingertips peeping out.

"*What happened?*" I gasped on seeing both casualties. Having settled on the Adrenaline Package for Executives, our organisation had made its valiant contribution to averting the latest one of its annual financial crises. As Stu had predicted, I managed to wriggle out of partaking in the corporate bonding event with laughable ease.

"Basically, it was the horse… I was horse riding… this horse… this horse hadn't been broken in properly… it threw me off. I think I might sue."

"Oh dear, Aston, that's terrible – I'm so sorry!"

"But you should feel more sympathy for the poor horse – the state it was in," whispered Crystal with a chuckle. "I'd say it had a perfectly honed self-preservation instinct; I mean, to be expected to carry all that weight."

According to Crystal and Stu, who gave me a low-down on the event, it had left a long trail of casualties in its wake. Apparently, Millie had decided to try jet skiing but, regrettably, had failed to realise how powerful the jet propulsion system of a watercraft could be. As a result, her craft shot high up into the air and, as it was executing the first of several somersaults, she was unceremoniously ejected before crashing into the waves. I was given to understand that her injuries included whiplash, several lacerations, severe bruising and friction burns plus a few other things I have forgotten.

Molly had attempted to do some white-water rafting but managed to overturn the raft, which hit her on the head, stripped her of all her acrylic nails and inflicted all manner of other injuries upon her person. At least she was the font of the most cutting-edge health and wellness advice so – unlike her *profits* of doom – would thus undoubtedly be able to look on the bright side of things: she could have been drowned, for example. Theo was scuba diving when this creature – he was unable to identify the culprit – swam right up to him and bit off a tip of his index finger. Ant tried mountain biking along a particularly challenging trail, came off, catapulted down a slope and broke all his extremities plus a few ribs. Thankfully, none of the fractures was open, but the bike was a complete write-off, and the man was now consigned to a wheelchair. Most of the other colleagues also sustained a catalogue of injuries ranging from entirely superficial to more major.

The most unusual mishap by far had undoubtedly befallen Hudson, who got extensive frostbite when his paragliding harness got sucked up to nearly 20,000 feet by a freak vortex. Happily, he managed to get back to earth before freezing to death, although he touched down in the Outer Hebrides, and they had to fly him back home in a Puma helicopter.

The most serious casualty, however, was Su Pine, whose rope snapped when she was bungee-jumping.

Luckily, she managed to land on a great big pile of rubber tyres, although they did have to call the fire brigade to cut her free from her rubbery trap, inside which she had become firmly lodged. Apparently, she resembled the Michelin Man who had overdone it on the tyres, with only the very top of her head sticking out. Unfortunately, one of the firefighters, a relative novice, was a tad too trigger-happy with his cutting device and was slicing through the tyres a little too enthusiastically. Anyway, the upshot was that she had to be hospitalised and was thus unable to attend our rebranding roll-out despite a three-line whip having been imposed on all FART's employees for the auspicious occasion.

The rest of our cluster got off comparatively lightly: Crystal slipped while gill scrambling and sustained some scratches to her wrist and an assortment of bruises, Stu got a rope burn in the course of abseiling – an injury not serious in itself but one which afflicted a rather tender part of his anatomy. Dew pulled an arm muscle while climbing, and Viv fell off a quad bike, dislocating her shoulder, which has now, happily, been put back where it belonged. Actually, that was the official version of events; she told me that it was, in fact, Mala – one of the few colleagues to have escaped the bedlam entirely unscathed – who, fired up by her competitive spirit, was trying to race her on her own quad bike and deliberately cut her up. Mindful of the three-line whip, I enquired of the more serious casualties, "So how are they going to get themselves to the Hilton?"

"They've already gone: they got them a fleet of ambulances."

Hilton's imposing conference hall did indeed resemble an accident and emergency department on a Friday night. I felt particularly sorry for the unfortunate Ant, who was looking like an Egyptian mummy in his gleaming wheelchair, which had been positioned by some half-wit right by a large tray with profiteroles. Poor man, I thought: for all I know, he might be dying to try one, but all his extremities are immobilised. I was in the process of wondering whether I should go over and feed him some when I heard a cheery, "Hi, Ali, hi, Crystal." I quickly turned round.

"Hello, Viv. I hope your shoulder is better." Having stayed overnight at the Hilton, Viv and Theo, the latter minus his fingertip, joined Crystal and me.

"Much better, thanks; at least I'm not missing any bits." Viv shot Theo a commiserative look.

"I did hear you'd had a rather adventurous day. Such events should carry a health warning, don't you think?"

"They certainly should, Ali. Oh, not again!"

"Absolutely, Viv. I wouldn't try anything like that ever again – no matter how serious the financial crisis."

"No, no, Ali, I mean all that food! I've just had a large breakfast."

The spread laid on by the Hilton was lavish, the tables straining to support the weight of gingerbread cakes, profiteroles, croissants, syrup-smothered pancakes, muffins, biscuits, fruit and a mind-bogglingly wide assortment of most intricate canapés. To wash it all down, we had tea, coffee, hot chocolate, Coca Cola, Pepsi Cola, mineral water – both still and sparkling – and orange, apple, mango and grapefruit juice. You could also ask for herbal teas, apparently.

I must say that I was suitably impressed. "Wow, Viv, they have gingerbread cakes and profiteroles – and look at those canapés."

"All the same."

"Morning, morning, morning, all." This came from Stu, who was sauntering towards us.

"How's your burn, Stu?"

"Not too bad, Ali. But I have to be careful in the bedroom."

"Oh, Stu: too much information!"

"That's exactly what my missus says: less information, more action – ho, ho, ho! So are we all suitably excited about today?"

"Can't contain myself, ha, ha, ha!" Crystal's laughter suggested that I might be in for another treat.

As if on cue, Nota entered the hall and, gliding towards the podium, adjusted her skirt and flicked her hair before seizing the microphone and saying into it with the gravity befitting the occasion, "One, two, three agendas for action, testing, testing. Morning, troops; please proceed to your seats; the delivery of the event is about to commence."

We duly joined the invalids, who had already been placed in their seats by more able-bodied colleagues. I noticed that the poor Ant's wheelchair remained stationed by the profiteroles. I hope he doesn't like them as much as I do, I thought.

"You will be cognisant that we have just completed GROPE – I mean our Great Rebranding Operation for Promoting Engagement – and are about to roll-out our new corporate identity. As you are about to perceive, it will be different, distinct and unique. It's yet another milestone in the past history of our distinguished, renowned and venerable organisation, and I'm sure we are all excited and enthusiastic about participating in this important, significant and momentous event. The delivery will be presided over by our Foremost Authoritarian, who will be joining us shortly – be upstanding, please."

Those colleagues who were physically capable of performing this manoeuvre did so with great enthusiasm, and the audience – barring the unfortunates whose hands had been rendered unusable by bandages, splinters or plaster casts – erupted into ecstatic applause.

With his circumference roughly the same as his height, the Foremost Authoritarian presented a sight to behold, his perfect roundness giving him the appearance of a huge ball. For a brief moment, I imagined him rolling gingerly on the grass during a game of golf or being shot up in the air in cricket. Or, perhaps, being used in this peculiar game beloved of the Saga generation which the lovely natives call bowls and which I'd never even heard of in Poland. I was completely transfixed. But then I was assailed by a rather unappetising thought: our Foremost Authoritarian with Nota – or with Bona. Or indeed with his wife. How... how exactly did... did this work? The image, however, was so frightful that I immediately had to banish it from my brain.

The Foremost Authoritarian regarded his vast audience with a justifiably proprietorial look, cleared his throat – probably more for a theatrical effect than out of any real need to expel a newt lurking therein – and opened the proceedings to the tune of Mozart's *Jupiter*

Symphony. "I am delighted, gratified and thrilled to see you all this morning, although I understand one or two colleagues are slightly below par. First of all, let me take this opportunity to congratulate you all on your bold, valiant and gallant efforts to avert our recent financial crisis. I'm sure you will be delighted, gratified and thrilled to hear that we have succeeded, although I was entirely confident we would: after all, we've never failed in the past."

This was greeted with another spontaneous round of applause, which included some unfamiliar-sounding thuds.

"What's that?" I whispered to Crystal.

"Sounds like somebody banging their plaster cast against something."

"As you are all undoubtedly aware, FART has been held in great esteem throughout the country since its very inception – *in great esteem* – because of our unrivalled, unparalleled and incomparable achievements."

Another burst of enthusiastic clapping and banging interrupted the proceedings, which were thus unable to resume for a little while.

"Those achievements are also fully appreciated, esteemed and relished by our sponsoring government department, which, however, is now different, dissimilar and distinct from that which was giving us our grant – I mean that which was supporting us in our monumental, momentous and meaningful endeavours – in the past. As you will appreciate, a new broom – I mean a new government – always wants to do things in ways which are innovative, pioneering and unprecedented. They have thus decided that we would be even more monumental, momentous and meaningful if we adopted a new corporate identity. And those who hold the purse strings – I mean those who support you in your monumental, momentous and meaningful endeavours – must always be heeded, obeyed and complied with."

At this point, the Foremost Authoritarian was interrupted by another prolonged burst of riotous cheering and clapping – and the odd thud. The rumpus over, he continued.

"Given that among our corporate values are openness, transparency and honesty, we launched a wide-ranging, extensive and comprehensive rebranding exercise, which, as you will all be aware, has just been completed. We are thus about to unveil our unique, original and groundbreaking corporate identity. To carry out the rebranding exercise, we commissioned the Delivery of Unique Names for Corporations and Enterprises. And we are delighted, gratified and thrilled to have been joined today by Mr Dim Wit, who is DUNCE's Creative Director." The Foremost Authoritarian fixed his gaze on the bald-headed gentleman sitting unassumingly at the end of the third row. "Mr Wit, would you please join me on the podium."

The gentleman in question stood up, turned first left and then right, offering us a few highly respectful bows in the process, and then, slightly hesitatingly, proceeded to the podium, where an empty chair was anticipating his arrival.

"Mr Wit has been instrumental in delivering our unique, original and groundbreaking corporate identity and has agreed to make time in his extremely busy schedule to join us on this memorable day. He will share with us his insights into the wide-ranging, extensive and comprehensive rebranding exercise undertaken by DUNCE. I am sure you will give a very warm, cordial and friendly welcome to Mr Wit."

Our great leader's touching confidence in his flock proved fully justified, for the floor was again roused into a tempestuous ovation. Mr Wit looked over the audience with a weak, somewhat lopsided, smile, which gave a passable impression of slight embarrassment. His unassuming demeanour made us instantly warm to him and only prolonged our applause. When the din finally died down, the Foremost Authoritarian handed over the proceedings to the distinguished guest with the words: "Mr Wit, please take the floor."

"Dim, please," said Dim outstretching his arms as if attempting to embrace the human ball before him.

"Dim, the floor is yours."

Dim stood up, bowed to the Foremost Authoritarian, bowed to the audience, wrung his hands in a manner suggesting slight nerves, which endeared him to us even more, and embarked on his exposition.

"As you will be aware, DUNCE has been extremely – *extremely* – fortunate to have been commissioned by FART to handle its rebranding and to deliver its new corporate identity. On behalf of everybody at DUNCE, it gives me immense pleasure to say that it's been a great honour and privilege – *great honour and privilege* – to deliver this commission."

This, clearly, called for another round of raucous

applause, and that's exactly what the friendly audience supplied.

"And now it's my great honour and privilege – *great honour and privilege* – to share with you some of the insights into this lengthy journey which has taken us to this critical juncture. As you will appreciate, every rebranding operation requires carrying out an extensive customer-facing consultative engagement with enabling stakeholders. Between you and I, our resources were stretched to breaking point because, roughly at the same time, PISS also took a corporate decision to rebrand. We then had to canvass opinion throughout the entire country, so it was necessary to devise a consultative engagement survey. We had distributed 1,236,963 copies, and the response rate was 77%, so we had a lot of analysing, diagnosing and decomposing to do. There were also – just a minute…"

Dim cast a quick glance at a piece of paper he was holding in his hand.

"There were also 349,427 focus groups, 139,112 engagement meetings, 58,149 face-to-face interviews, 12,498 brainst… I mean thought-showering sessions, 4,378 rebranding conventions, 943 in-depth discussion groups and 398 conferences."

The audience gasped and rewarded Dim with a round of appreciative applause for all his troubles, with the Foremost Authoritarian enthusiastically joining in. Between you and *me* – definitely not between you and *I* – even I couldn't help being impressed by the extent of DUNCE's consultation. Dim was now in full flow.

"And the results were as follows: 81% of respondents

felt that 'foremost' should be replaced with 'supreme', 'dominant', 'paramount', 'preeminent' or 'superior'; 69% wanted 'authority' replaced with 'fraternity', 'board', 'institution', 'institute' or 'corporation'; 56% opted for 'talibanisation', 'extremisation' or 'fanatisation' instead of 'radicalisation', with 44% favouring the reinstatement of the previous 'regulation'; and, finally, 75% wanted 'transfiguration', 'transmutation', 'metamorphosis' or 'transition' in place of 'transformation'. The breakdown into the individual percentages can be found in my comprehensive report, which I have submitted to the Foremost Authoritarian. There was, of course, a range of other recommendations, but they were too outlandish to be taken seriously."

While the audience was in the throes of another ovation, I wondered what could possibly be more outlandish than 'talibanisation' or 'fanatisation'. But I have to admit that I couldn't wait to hear what our unique, original and groundbreaking corporate identity was going to be so continued to listen intently. Dim continued.

"I'm delighted to announce that your organisation's new corporate identity now reflects the lofty values you all stand for, your audacious direction of travel and the government's visionary road map to prosperity and economic miracle."

At this point, Dim paused for effect, and who could blame him? We all held our collective breath – when I say all, I mean those whose ribs hadn't been broken, of course – and stared intently at the projector screen behind Dim. After forty-or-so seconds of lapping up the suspense, Dim bent over the laptop, which was an essential piece of equipment on all similar occasions, and projected the eagerly anticipated slide onto the screen behind. The slide read:

FARTED

Rendered in an enormous red font, FARTED was surrounded by what uncannily resembled yellowish splashes. Luckily for Crystal, Viv, Stu and me, the huge gasp which issued from the audience was quickly followed by a burst of the wildest applause I had ever found myself in the midst of, drowning out the hysterical laughter which each of us was trying to strangle with both hands – not entirely successfully, I suspect.

There were cheers, there were shouts, there were whoops, there were whistles, there were squawks, there were honks, there were claps, there were rattles, there were thuds, and somebody even threw a party popper. Amid the sounds of the tumult, I could clearly discern: "Awesome, I'm liking it!"… "Jolly good, jolly good!"… "Aye, aye, aye!"… "Gucci!"… "Sick!"… "Cool beans!" I looked at the Foremost Authoritarian and could see that he was clapping so hard he resembled round-shaped grass jelly wobbling all over the podium.

When I was finally able to speak, I whispered to Crystal, "What are these… these yellow blobs?"

"They look like splashes, don't they?"

"That's exactly what I thought."

Finally, with the audience spent, the Foremost Authoritarian was able to move the proceedings forward. "I'm delighted, gratified and thrilled that our new corporate identity has been so well received. Do colleagues have any questions for Dim?"

"What are these… these yellow… thingies?" bravely enquired Crystal.

"They are stars."

"They are *stars?*"

"They most certainly are; you might need stronger glasses."

"In actual fact, I'm booked in for Friday."

"Good, good. Stars symbolise the aspirations of our young people: all our young people's dream is to reach for the stars."

"Is it now?" sniggered Viv, albeit in a whisper.

"And, with your help, I'm sure they will be able to," continued Dim.

"But what… what exactly does our new name stand for?" asked Val, albeit rather tentatively. Talk about slow on the uptake.

"The Foremost Authority for the Radicalisation of Transformation *in Education*. That's what your sponsoring government department decided you should be called. In the interests of honesty, openness and transparency. These are your core corporate values, I believe."

Some of us couldn't believe our ears, but it was our Theo who had the courage to ask: "*Decided?* Our new name was decided *by the government?*"

"Naturally."

"But what… what about your rebranding exercise – this wide-ranging consultative engagement survey and everything else?"

"Oh, that's standard practice in the public sector: you must always do this, so that nobody can accuse you of not consulting stakeholders. Am I right, Mr Morphic?" This question was, of course, directed at the Foremost Authoritarian, who gave a deep nod and swiftly took possession of the mike – an operation performed with the skill of Ronaldo on a football pitch.

"Absolutely right, correct and veracious, Dim. We've covered our back while, at the same time, protecting, shielding and safeguarding our government grant. Any more questions?"

"But... but what about this... this comprehensive consultation report mentioned by Mr Wit?" asked Stu. "As I understand it, adding education to our name – I mean to our corporate identity – hadn't been suggested by the respondents – I mean by the enabling stakeholders – so what if people read the report and...?"

"Nobody will read the report," interjected the Foremost Authoritarian rather abruptly. "We have designated it as highly classified. It will be declassified in fifty years' time, but I don't think we need to worry about this. Any further questions?"

Amid more riotous applause, no other questions were forthcoming, which enabled the Foremost Authoritarian to bring the whole shebang to a close.

"I'm delighted, gratified and thrilled to see such lively interest from the floor. We are, of course, going to stage a series of launch events throughout the country to explain the visions, missions and ideals embodied in our new corporate identity. But man does not live by ideals alone: brunch is served in the Saffron Restaurant on the mezzanine floor."

***

As always, Crystal, Viv, Stu and I made straight for the salads, which usually had the fewest takers. On this occasion, the longest queue by far was that for the spiced pork belly stuffed with prunes, although braised lamb shanks, one-pan duck with Savoy cabbage and juniper pork fillet also attracted a decent following. I was relieved to see that Val Erian was feeding Ant chicken, goat's cheese and cherry tomato bake, although, to tell you the truth, I would have been just as relieved to see him being fed *anything* – as long as the poor man didn't have to starve. I was also delighted, gratified and thrilled that the unfortunate Hudson, whose frostbitten mitts were out of commission, was also being attended to.

Over a plate of gravadlax with quail eggs nesting on a bed of tossed green salad (with no dressing), I looked at my friends with deep, misty-eyed fondness.

"Is it me, or are they all completely bonkers?"

"Relax: it's not you, Ali." Stu's chortle was even more reassuring than his words.

"Yep, it's a madhouse," concurred Crystal. "Just as well that we all have a sense of humour."

"I have a madhouse joke for you," said Stu. "An American takes a sightseeing tour around London. While looking at the sights, he asks the guide: 'Why is everything so small here? Look at this building, for example. In America, it would be ten times as big.' The guide replies: 'I completely agree, sir. That's the madhouse,' ho, ho, ho!"

"Particularly with Trump, Vance and Musk running amok over there," agreed Viv. "By the way, did Dim say they were also rebranding PISS? Shall we tell them what their new corporate identity is going to be?"

As we were laughing, we saw Aston stagger in our direction on his reinforced crutches, with Millie limping beside. They were both supported by Mala, who was trying her best to prevent either from toppling. Deep down, she probably was a kind lady, I thought. Jock was pushing Ant's wheelchair, with Delia, Dew and Delle following on behind. When they all joined us, I looked at Aston and was somewhat surprised by an uncharacteristically solemn expression on his face.

Aston motioned us to one side with the words: "I have something important to tell you."

We all looked at him expectantly.

"A few of you will be aware that, shortly after Delia joined us, I entered her for the General Certificate in Administrative Capacities for Digital Horizons. But I thought it best if we kept it from her; assessment was by continuous observation by me because it is a practical qualification, so she didn't have to sit any written exams. And I have just completed assessing the final module of her programme."

We all looked at Delia, who appeared completely stunned.

"So… so what's the result, Aston?" asked Viv.

Aston paused for a bit - undoubtedly to amplify the effect of his forthcoming announcement - before jubilantly announcing: "She passed; many congratulations, Delia!"

In that instant, I forgot all about his greengrocers' apostrophes, mangled punctuation, mutilated spelling and other linguistic misdemeanours - nothing beats a warm heart, after all.

I can honestly say that our applause was every bit as riotous as that delivered earlier in the conference room, although there were many fewer of us. We showered the overjoyed Delia with hugs and kisses and, I am not embarrassed to admit, shed quite a few tears. Happy tears.